ADRENALIN
RIDE

ADRENALIN RIDE

Pam Withers

Dedicated to Avril and Roger Withers

Text copyright © 2004 by Pam Withers
Walrus Books, an imprint of Whitecap Books
Third printing, 2008

Edited by Carolyn Bateman
Proofread by Elizabeth McLean
Cover and interior design by Roberta Batchelor
Cover photograph by Annika Ridington

Printed and bound in Canada

Library and Archives of Canada Cataloguing in Publication

Withers, Pam
  Adrenalin ride / Pam Withers.

(Take it to the extreme)
ISBN 1-55285-604-6
ISBN 978-1-55285-604-8

  I. Title. II. Series: Withers, Pam. Take it to the extreme.
PS8595.I8453A64 2004   jC813'.6   C2004-904186-X

The publisher acknowledges the financial support of the Canada
Council for the Arts, the British Columbia Arts Council, and the
Government of Canada through the Book Publishing Industry
Development Program (BPIDP). Whitecap Books also acknowledges
the financial support of the Province of British Columbia through the
Book Publishing Tax Credit.

We are committed to protecting the environment and to the responsible use of natural
resources. We are acting on this commitment by working with suppliers and printers to phase
out our use of paper produced from ancient forests. This book is printed by Webcom on 100%
recycled (40% post-consumer) paper, processed chlorine free and printed with vegetable-based
inks. We are working with Markets Initiative (www.marketsiniative.org) on this project.

Contents

1   Flying Circus

Sweat trickled from Jake Evans's brow inside his full-face helmet as he clattered down a ladder bridge, leaned into a turn, and prepared to launch from the top of the five-foot drop ahead of him. It dribbled down the back of his neck and crept into dark, smelly places under his body armor as he gripped his handlebars tighter and caught some air on the steep mountain face. Then, with the fullest concentration he'd ever mustered in all his fifteen years, he pulled up on his handlebars and willed his rear tire to hit the transition — the dusty run-out — just so. In mountain-biking videos, this was the moment where riders lifted their feet off the pedals and kicked their heels before remounting and touching earth with an exuberant victory smile. But Jake wasn't being filmed, and unlike his friend Peter Montpetit, who had disappeared ahead of him ten minutes ago, he had no aspirations of being a video star. Just getting down this outrageous piece of mountain with bike and body intact would be fine with him today.

Yes! A perfect touchdown, everything still upright and operational, never mind the streams of sweat now running freely down his torso as if squeezed from his pores by the body-jarring landing. Jake braked, pulled to the side of the trail, and surveyed the forest around him. So where was Peter, and how the heck had he talked Jake into riding the Flying Circus trail anyway? The wildest ride in Vancouver, Canada's North Shore Mountains was way beyond their abilities, as Jake had guessed. But that was Peter for you, a go-for-it guy with a contagious level of exuberance and daring.

"Peter!" Jake shouted into the quiet, sweet-scented cedars, searching for his best friend. No answer, and no sign of him. But that was Peter through and through, too. Impulsive to the max and easily distracted from thoughts of safety by the excitement of the moment. Especially when trying out a brand-new full-suspension bike. Lucky brat, Jake thought, patting his own trusty, rusty hard-tail with only a modicum of jealousy. Never mind. Peter had said that Jake could try his out when they reached the lower slopes today, and that was good enough for Jake. Good enough, that is, if they reached the lower slopes with no broken bones.

"Peter!" Jake tried again, annoyed at being left behind. Hopping back on his bike, he took off down the tree-root-riddled trail, eyes on a long, narrow log ahead. He had to cross it to reach the point where the trail continued on the other side. Jake was halfway across, trying not to glimpse the forest floor below, when he felt his bike begin to wobble.

"Jake, old buddy," he heard Peter shout from the far side. "Go for it. You can do it."

Too late. Jake's instincts flashed him a signal to jump off the log bridge before tipping off it in a less-controlled fashion. He braked to a stop, lifted both feet off the pedals, and hurled himself through the air like a gymnast. At the same instant, he pushed his bike away so that he wouldn't fall on top of it — or it on him — when he reached the gully below. Then he tucked for a roll to help soften the impact of the fall, thankful for the soft cedar-bark and needle-strewn ground. Hardly had he come to a halt when Peter, leaping and skidding down the gully toward him, let out a volley of cheers.

"What a dismount, Jake, my man! Perfect way to fall off a log ride if you *have* to fall off a log ride. Good thing it wasn't a foot or two higher, though, hey? That would've broken an ankle for sure. I know,

I know, you're blaming me for hauling you onto this trail, but what a rush! I made it across, Jake, and you almost did."

He jogged over to where Jake's bike had fallen and picked it up, blond curls stiff with sweat, smile lighting up his face. "And your bike's totally okay, except for a bent brake lever." Jake held his tongue as Peter fiddled with the part so vigorously that it seemed sure to break off if not already beyond repair. "We'll be okay, Jake. We're done with the worst stuff now, I think."

As if he knew anything about where they were or what still lay ahead. "I'm not sure which is worse," Jake replied with a grin. "The Flying Circus on my own or listening to your motor-mouthing when I do catch up with you."

"Aw, suck it up, old buddy. I was barely ahead of you. And this is *fun* stuff, *crazy*. Should we do The Shore every day the next two weeks? Or tackle Hidden Pleasures on Vedder Mountain near your house tomorrow? This run's awesome. We haven't got anything like it in Seattle, that's for sure. Here I am, looking at two weeks' vacation with you, Jake. Just you and me and whatever we get up to. Like before I moved away. And look what's right here in your backyard!"

"Peter," Jake pointed out with exaggerated patience as he removed his helmet to run a hand through his sweaty, unruly brown mop, "this is not my backyard.

This is the North Shore of Vancouver, and as you well know, it was nearly a two-hour drive from my house in Chilliwack to get here, courtesy of your cousin Tyler Baxter, who thinks we're on an easier trail. Anyway, I might get called into work sometime the next two weeks. But we'll have a blast no matter what we get up to, and I think it's great your parents let you loose up here for two weeks. One day down, thirteen to go."

"Hey, don't say thirteen. That's bad luck," Peter said. "And how is your slave-labor job at Sam's Adventure Tours these days? Washed any buses lately? Swept any equipment-shed floors? Patched any torn rafts?"

Jake, knowing Peter was just jealous that he had a paying job, took this in good humor. "Sam's having a slow season, which is why I keep having to wait to get called in. Otherwise, everything is great except for Ron not being there this summer."

"Ron Gabanna, the shady, muscle-bound grump who liked his beer a little too much? I'm surprised he lasted more than a season. Always struck me as a drifter, kinda scary."

Jake smiled. "Just 'cause he likes me, and not you, and can whoop you at any athletic feat, doesn't make him scary, Peter." Even as he spoke, though, Jake's memory flashed back to the whitewater rafting and kayaking trip in northern British Columbia on which the three had last been together. He remembered how Peter had "borrowed" Ron's kayak without permission. When Ron had given chase by raft, the guide had ended up going over a thirty-foot waterfall that had nearly killed him. And he'd lost the raft. The incident had put the entire expedition in jeopardy. Yes, Ron had been drunk at the time, and, yes, Ron and Peter had sort of made up when all was said and done. But even without that misadventure, there was no natural affinity between Ron, the hard-edged, temperamental, world-traveled outdoor guide, and Peter, whose high energy and spoiled-rich-kid personality could grate on anyone at times. Then again, Jake smirked, that nonstop exuberance was what made Peter cool, and it had gotten them out of tight spots as well as into them.

"Still," Jake decided aloud as he turned to Peter, "I know you like Ron no matter what you say."

"Maybe," Peter responded as he sprinted up the slope, retrieved his fancy bike, and raced down the trail ahead, gold-colored helmet shining in the sun. No matter what sport Peter did, he always bought a gold helmet.

Within half an hour, the two boys were waiting outside the café that was their designated pickup point. Jake pressed his dirt-spattered face against the café's window and licked his dry lips at the sight of a stack of giant blueberry muffins. He could almost taste them, they were so close.

"Can't believe I left my wallet in your cousin's car," he moaned.

Peter cupped his hands around his eyes to follow Jake's stare. "Watch my bike and look out for Tyler. I'll be right back," he instructed.

Jake turned and scanned the parking lot, waving when he saw the red sports car with the sturdy rear bicycle rack pull near. As Jake lifted the first dirt-caked bike onto the rack, he was interrupted by the appearance of a muffin under his nose.

"One blueberry muffin, sized extra-large for a Flying Circus survivor," Peter announced.

"You're the greatest," Jake replied. He secured the bike, then hopped into the back seat of the car to eat the muffin, nodding to Peter's cousin Tyler. Reaching for the water bottle tucked into his backpack behind him, he cursed as the bag toppled over, spilling its contents into his lap. "Shoot. Wrong bag," he muttered, stuffing Peter's shirt and wallet back into the sack.

Even as his teeth sank into the muffin, though, he couldn't help thinking, "How did Peter buy that muffin without his wallet?" With loose change in his shorts pocket, he hoped, but even the muffin melting in his mouth failed to chase away an unsettled feeling. Had Peter taken up stealing?

"Jake, Jake, phone for you!" his sister Alyson was calling from the front steps of their small bungalow as Tyler's car pulled up.

"Thanks, Al," Jake said as he leaped out and took the phone from his younger sister. "Hello?"

"Hey, kid. This is Ron. Ron Gabanna," came a deep voice through the line.

"Ron?" Jake's eyes widened as he pressed the receiver against his ear and moved through a swinging gate to a lawn chair in their small backyard. "No way. We were just talking about you. Where are you? What's happening? Are you coming back to Sam's Adventure Tours?"

"Nope. But I'm doin' something that might interest you. Starting up a mountain bike tour company in the Interior — a few hours east of you. And I need some strong backs and hands to help me finish the bike trails. I'm kinda behind schedule. Ten days' work. Pay's good and comes with a free bike while you're here — new, top-of-the-line full-suspension in case you were wondering. I bet you can handle one of those, eh? And what about your Seattle buddy, Peter? Think he'd be keen?"

Jake's jaw slackened an inch. He couldn't think what to say. So he let Ron ramble on with details. His chin dropped further when Ron named his salary: twice what he was earning at Sam's on the days he did get called in, plus food, camping gear, and bus fare. There were only two catches: He had to drop everything and catch a bus to Keremeos in south-central British Columbia within the next two days, and he wasn't supposed to mention Ron's new enterprise to Sam's Adventure Tours staff.

"They might see me as competition," Ron explained.

"Ron," Jake said into the phone as Peter appeared in the backyard with their bikes and began spraying them down with the garden hose, "I'll call you back later on tonight, okay? Gotta get my mom's permission and talk to Peter, but, well, how could we say no? What's your phone number? Thanks, Ron."

Peter was eyeing Jake suspiciously as he shut off the water and accepted two glasses of iced tea from Alyson, who'd appeared on the back deck.

"Perfect, Alyson. What a gal. Now out with it, Jake, you little sneak. What do you have to check with me about, and what can't you say no to involving Ron Gabanna?"

2   Garage Full of Bikes

Jake gazed out the bus window as scenery blinked by and marveled that he was headed east on an unexpected adventure guaranteed to give him some badly needed spending money. Peter's sleeping head sagged against his shoulder in the mid-morning light.

He could hardly believe the events of the past fifteen hours. One late-afternoon phone call to Peter's parents in Seattle. One animated discussion with his mother when she'd arrived home from her day job, before she could leave for her evening job. Twenty minutes spent crowded in front of the computer in Jake's bedroom with Peter, Alyson, and his mother peering over his shoulder as he calculated bus departure times and rates. An excited call back to Ron, who booked their five-hour bus ride to Keremeos. A message left on Sam's Adventure Tours' answering machine saying he would be unavailable for two weeks. And, after his mom left, a late evening trip to the grocery store, from which Peter had emerged with several bags of pepperoni sticks.

"We've been caught out before with no food in the backcountry," he'd pronounced.

"Now there's an understatement," Alyson had commented, all too well acquainted with the boys' previous misadventures.

Even though he and Peter had had to get up before dawn for their early morning delivery to the bus station, Jake was psyched to be going somewhere new. He recalled the ride to the bus station, and the requisite public hugs from his mom and Alyson. Although Peter had guffawed when Alyson had pressed an empty jar with holes punched in the lid into Jake's hands before he boarded, Jake was touched. She wanted to expand her butterfly collection and trusted him to bring back an exotic specimen or two. Most guys Jake knew considered younger sisters a pain in the butt, and Peter, being an only child, couldn't be expected to understand. But Jake had a special place in his heart for Alyson, three years younger. Maybe they hadn't been close before his dad had taken off on them after a fight with their mom a few years back. Maybe he'd taken her for granted, considered her a nuisance, before then. But for Jake, the painful blow of not hearing from his father since could only be softened by trying to be a sort-of dad as well as older brother to Alyson. And if that meant hunting butterflies while building a bike trail in the wilderness, that's just the way it was.

As for his mom, she may not have wanted him to go, may have had doubts even when he explained that Ron was a responsible senior guide at Sam's Adventure Tours. ("Ha! Responsible for guarding his beer supply, maybe," Peter had laughed later.) But the money Jake would be earning had turned it all in his favor, fast. Even with one and a half jobs, his mom was always struggling to pay the bills. Anything he could earn took weight off her shoulders. So in the end, he'd won her reluctant approval.

As the bus sped over the mountain pass, Jake watched endless stands of lush green trees travel by. After an hour, the trees thinned out, the tumbling creek beside the highway became a wide, boulder-studded river, and rounded hills of dry grass appeared between greener slopes. Soon, orchards elbowed onto the landscape, interspersed with cattle, sheep, and horse ranches, all backdropped by spectacular mountain peaks in every direction. It all looked so hot and dry compared with the west side of the mountains. In fact, Jake reflected, the edge of desert country in the middle of the driest summer on record could only mean sweltering temperatures. But given the money he and Peter would be earning, Jake would do hard labor in any conditions. Ron must really be counting on his bike tours taking off to be able to pay that. And they probably would, given that a popular provincial backcountry area had agreed to allow biking within its boundaries for the first time ever, and Ron alone had won the permit.

"I'm just a very persuasive, patient guy, what can I say?" he'd boasted over the phone.

Beside Jake, Peter stirred, sat up, and looked out the window. "We're over the pass, I see. How long till Keremeos?" he asked with a yawn. "Where the heck is Keremeos again?"

"Five hours east of Vancouver, near the Canadian/ U.S. border," Jake replied, unzipping his backpack and yanking out a page he'd downloaded from the Web the evening before. "Population 1,200, nearest town to Cathedral Provincial Park, which is 33,000 hectares of mountains. Highest point, 2,600 metres."

"Translated to American, that's — let's see — around 80,000 acres and 8,500 feet elevation," Peter calculated, face breaking into a self-congratulatory smile. "Hmmm, gimme that map. If it's on the U.S. border, I want to know where we *really* are. Okay, 150 miles northeast of Seattle. Hey, we're directly above Winthrop, Washington. That's where my grandparents live. Did I ever tell you about my grandpa? He was one of the first smokejumpers."

"Smoke what?"

"Smokejumpers. The team that parachutes into forest fires to help battle them. First ones to the fire. They wear special fireproof suits. It's way more dangerous than any other firefighting job."

"Sounds scary. Guess that's where you get your feet-first, brain-last personality," Jake teased. They laughed and arm-wrestled until the woman in the next seat told them to settle down, after which they dug into their backpacks for some junk food.

"Gotta stock up before that mean old Ron takes us to his slave camp," said Peter.

By the time the bus had pulled into a small station, the early afternoon sun was beating down on the parched landscape, all but sucking oxygen from the air. They recognized Ron immediately. He was leaning against a beat-up white pickup truck, mesh vest and running shorts showing off the twenty-eight-year-old's tall, super-muscular build. Not the all-for-show steroids sort of guy, but a true athlete, Jake reflected with a surge of warmth for the man. A portable stereo was slung around his waist, and he was jiving to its tunes. His greasy blond hair was pulled back into a ponytail, and his earlobes seemed to have acquired a few more earrings since the last time Jake had seen him. His blue eyes lit up when he saw them. He ambled over, switched off his music, and ran a fond hand through Jake's hair while nodding politely at Peter.

"Welcome to Keremeos, boys, old gold minin' place. These days, fruit stands outnumber bars, and black bears wander the orchards. And you've just joined the finest bike touring company ever to hit provincial parkland."

"Happy to be here," Jake replied, unable to wipe a big smile off his face as his eyes darted up and down the main street to take it all in. His feet were itching to climb onto the brand-new bike that would soon be his. They threw their small packs into the back of Ron's truck and squeezed onto the worn vinyl front seat, which felt as hot as a branding iron against the backs of their legs after the air-conditioned bus. A bumpy, ten-minute ride at high speed brought them to a tiny, rundown, boxy white house on the edge of town. Pieces of its siding were missing and there was no lawn to speak of. Just a fenceless patch of sun-burnt grass.

"Got lemonade in the fridge for you, but first you'll wanna see my garage," Ron said with a wink as he cut the engine and hopped out. Jake sprinted to Ron's side and smiled as the big man rested a hand on his shoulder. Peter, whose wariness of Ron seemed to have tied his tongue, followed behind. Two massive padlocks secured the front of the garage, Jake noticed, but Ron was leading them to a steel door at the side, where a triple set of locks took a few minutes to open. That's a lot of locks for an ordinary old garage, Jake thought. As the door swung open and Ron hit a light switch, Jake caught his breath. Before them was an entire fleet of brand-new mountain bikes, close to twenty by Jake's count, each outfitted with custom nylon saddlebags in sturdy, army-camouflage nylon. But Peter, the bike expert, wasn't impressed.

"You said we'd have full-suspension bikes," he complained. "These are hard-tails — with saddlebags to get in the way of good jumps and stuff."

"Settle down, Peter. These are for the tourists. Your bikes are over here." Ron strode to a dusty corner and pulled a string below a bare light bulb. Jake grinned as Peter dashed over to touch the two bikes as if they were the Holy Grail.

"Dual-crown forks and a four-bar linkage — eight inches of travel front and rear!" he marveled. "Better than mine. Cost you a bundle," he said, directing a steady, almost accusing gaze at Ron.

"They'll do, then, I take it?" Ron replied with a glint in his eyes as he pulled the light cord again and pressed a large hand against Peter's back to lead him out of the garage. "You get better ones 'cause you're building trail, not hauling stuff in bike bags, which would get tangled in full-suspension bikes' gears. Mine's the same as yours, except for having single-crown forks. Now let's get down to business."

Jake's head throbbed from the heat despite Ron's iced lemonade and sandwiches. His eyes kept threatening to close as Ron went over plans, how they'd be riding up the mountain later that evening and camping at a site already established with tools, tents, sleeping bags, and food.

"Why not leave now?" asked the ever impulsive Peter.

"It's too hot," Ron replied, his voice curt and eyes shifting to the only window in the messy living room where they were gathered. Messy was hardly the word for it, thought Jake, gazing glassy-eyed from his worn easy chair to the stacks of yellowed newspapers, a table covered with maps, and corners filled with overflowing garbage bags. Dumbbells cluttered the floor beneath the scarred kitchen counter and empty beer bottles covered every other available space in the kitchen. Cocking his groggy head to peer into the sole bedroom of the little house, Jake was reminded of a black-and-white postcard of a cowboy's cabin: sagging mattress, worn boots pulled up to the foot of the bed, and, hanging from hooks on the wall, backpacks — the modern-day equivalent of chaps and a gun belt.

He muted out Ron and Peter's conversation about

wildlife in the park and let his head fall back. The last two things he registered before drifting into sleep were the way Ron kept glancing at his watch and the living room's only wall decoration. It was an old photo of Ron as a teen, glowing with pride, hunting rifle in one hand, the other holding up a freshly shot cougar. Beside him, one hand proudly locked on Ron's shoulder, stood a man who so resembled Ron today, it could only have been his father.

3   Base Camp

A slamming door and the sound of raised voices awakened Jake. Ron, face flushed, was stomping into the room with Peter, head bowed, in tow. Jake sat up and rubbed his eyes as Ron stood before him, hands on his hips, eyes flashing.

"Lucky for your buddy that I know the hardware store owner," Ron declared. His booming voice hurt Jake's ears. "Tried shoplifting a Swiss army knife while I was gettin' some last-minute supplies. Not a great start to a new job. The manager was going to press charges till I had a talk with him. I managed to stop him from giving Peter his first police record. But my condition for doing that is that he stays honest here-on in."

Ron, whose temper had always frightened Jake a little, seemed to be staring at Jake as if he was responsible. Jake squirmed in his seat and shifted his eyes to

Peter, who was studying the floor. So Jake's hunch about the muffin had been right. This was a new, unsettling, and unexpected change in Peter. Jake was going to have to figure out how to ask Peter about it. For now, though, Peter wouldn't even meet his gaze. Jake looked back to Ron, who tossed a plastic bag of newly purchased items on the table and softened a bit.

"I'm gonna assume it won't happen again. Not much to steal up in the park anyway. Sorry, Jake, didn't mean to wake you up like that. Not your fault. Let's get movin'. It's time."

Jake jumped up and grabbed his pack as Peter slunk to the kitchen to refill his water bottle and Ron stomped out. The sound of keys clicking open the garage door propelled Jake down the front steps to help Ron load the bicycles into the back of the pickup and toss their three small backpacks into the corners. Then Ron fastened a tarp over the top, neatly hiding everything beneath, returned to the house to lock up, and hopped into the driver's seat.

"Do you always cover them with a tarp?" Jake asked, curious. Something about that seemed strange.

"Yup. No point in gettin' 'em dusty before we're on the trail."

Didn't make sense, but Jake shrugged and sat in the uncomfortable middle seat to help ease tensions between Ron and Peter as the truck roared to life and set off through town. Although thankful for the release from the day's heat, Jake couldn't help worrying a little about how late they were starting out. Surely it would be dark by the time they made it to the camp Ron had described, and if any problems arose along the way, they had nothing but the foil-thin emergency blankets and water-filter pump Ron had added to the boys' packs of clothes. In fact, following Ron's earlier phone instructions, the boys had brought nothing but fleece jackets and trousers, underclothing, thermals, raingear, water bottles, headlamps, helmets, bike repair essentials, a book each, and some snack food. They were still wearing the shorts and T-shirts in which they'd arrived. It struck Jake as risky, traveling so lightly so near to sunset in a wilderness area. But Ron's directions had been firm: "No cameras, binoculars, compasses, cellphones, or sundries."

Sundries. A funny word for miscellaneous, extra stuff, Jake decided. He settled back, making no effort to draw Peter into his and Ron's sporadic conversation. Let him suffer if he was going to kick off their trip on the wrong foot, Jake fumed. Shoplifting was dumb. And how dare he do it in Ron's town, behind Ron's back, and put Ron in a bad mood before they even started. Did he realize he owed Ron big-time now, for saving him from a police record? But what really bugged Jake was how he couldn't imagine Peter suddenly becoming dishonest. How else was Peter changing that Jake wasn't seeing? He didn't like to think of them growing apart. They'd been best friends since kindergarten, except for a short spell after Peter had moved to Seattle.

Jake placed his hand on the radio knob while throwing a questioning glance at Ron. It was Ron's truck, after all. Ron, more relaxed now, gave him a thumbs-up with an indulgent smile and even pretended to know the words of the songs that blasted them, along with tons of dust, for the next hour's travel.

"Ashnola River," Peter read a road sign aloud when he finally found his voice. Another sign came into view. "'Cathedral Provincial Park. No dogs or bikes.' Guess they'll have to change that one soon."

"Very soon," Ron said, voice stoked with pride. Was it pride? Or was his voice just louder than natural? Jake wondered why the sign hadn't been changed already.

"Too bad we didn't bring our kayaks. Looks just right for some radical whitewater paddling," Peter ventured.

"Too low," Ron replied. "This region's been cryin' for rain for weeks. The whole forest is a tinderbox, and the Ashnola's only good with a little more lubrication on those rocks."

They drove past a big wooden sign announcing

Cathedral Lakes Lodge, which perked Jake up. "A lodge up top, eh? Why don't we take that road, Ron?"

"'Cause we ain't that lazy!" he joked as he stepped on the gas pedal. "Rich tourists go up that road in an open-air Unimog, which is a tough version of a Hummer, and get a glass of wine served to 'em to calm their nerves when they get to the top. It's a very rough four-wheel-drive road; my truck wouldn't take it. Anyhow, I don't have permission. *Yet,*" he added loudly.

If he had permission to build a bike trail, why wouldn't he have access to the park's only road? Jake wondered, reflecting for a moment on how Ron had urged them not to tell anyone they were building a trail, and had hidden the bikes beneath a tarp.

"But we can visit the lodge once we get up there, right?" Jake pressed. "Maybe they sell ice cream cones?"

Ron snorted. "We ain't goin' near there, and they don't sell ice cream cones to smelly bikers or hikers. They do have a fancy fireplace with mounted antlers and bookcases all over the walls, and a hot tub, and kitchen staff," he teased. "I've gotten close enough to peek in and see that. But I've never been invited in, and we'll be the other side of some peaks, anyhow. You wait to get rich before you try going there."

"I'm going to be rich some day," Peter announced.

As if he isn't already, Jake thought, with a pilot for a dad and a flight attendant for a mom.

"No doubt," Ron sneered.

"I'm going to be a prime-time television anchor-man or an actor."

"Well, got the looks and cockiness for it," Ron allowed. "But don't go gettin' yourself a police record or it won't happen."

That shut Peter down quickly, Jake noticed, figuring his buddy deserved it. Peter turned and stared out the window, gulping water from his water bottle as if forgetting it had to last him several hours up a steep trail.

When Ron finally slowed his vehicle and parked it in a place Jake figured no thieves — or anyone else — would ever find, it took only seconds for the boys to lift their bikes from the truck and follow Ron in wheeling them across slippery boulders in the Ashnola to where an established if somewhat disused hiking trail started: one easily negotiated by bike.

By now, the sun was near setting, and Jake watched Ron check his watch for the hundredth time that day. "Ride where you can, walk 'em where it's too steep, boys," he directed before slinging his powerful legs over his crossbar and pulling away from them at an impressive speed.

Although he only occasionally rode out of sight,

Ron remained far enough ahead over the next three hours that Jake and Peter were able to talk in private snatches, especially when the rocky trail forced them to push their heavy bikes for long periods, which was often.

"It'll be fun coming down this stuff," Peter observed, wiping sweat from his brow and glancing back down the mountain. "And good thing we didn't have to do this earlier this afternoon, or we'd have collapsed of heat stroke."

"Actually, I don't get that bit," Jake confided. "He's going to have us sweating all day tomorrow on trail construction. We could've made it up here earlier. In fact, I'm worried about not getting there before dark. Isn't this the time of day that bears wander around?"

"You're always worrying," Peter said. "You were asleep when we discussed wildlife. There are no bears in this park. They were hunted out years ago, and anyway, the orchards around Keremeos are easier pickings than up top, where it's too dry and the growing season is too short for berries to grow."

"Well, any other animals to know about?" Jake searched the gathering shadows in the dry forest around them.

"Mule deer, mountain goats, bighorn sheep, chipmunks, squirrels, pikas, and marmots. I s'pose a goat or sheep could butt you off a mountain cliff if you turned your back, or a chipmunk could nibble on your little toe."

"What about cougars?" Jake pressed.

"Oh yeah, there are cougars, but they're more interested in deer than people."

"I've heard of cougars stalking and killing people. Remember that news story about those two mountain bikers who were followed for miles before a cougar leaped and got one?" Jake shivered as he pulled his bike over a fallen branch.

"Yup. Sank its teeth into the back of his neck. Killed him instantly. The other guy saved himself by lifting his bike above his head so that he looked tall and ferocious, and the cougar took off," Peter recalled. "Smart rider. Stupid cat."

Jake turned to stare at Peter. "Stupid cat? Is that all you can say? That was a horrible case. And you weren't going to admit there are cougars around here?"

"Jake, you worry too much. Hardly anyone ever sees a cougar, let alone gets attacked by one. That was a weird, freak thing, and it was on Vancouver Island, where they keep building houses in places cougars have always hunted. You won't see a cougar around here. They stay way clear of humans if they can. Don't even bring it up again, worrywart."

Jake agreed that it was time to change the subject.

He slowed the pace at which they were riding. "So, how're things in Seattle? You were kind of down on the city the last time we talked."

"Yeah, school sucked last year 'cause the two guys I hung out with most moved away."

"Right, that can really suck. I remember," Jake needled, remembering the crisis he went through when Peter and his family left Chilliwack for Seattle.

"The guys I've been hanging with since are a little crazy."

"Like, fun-crazy or too-wild crazy?"

"They steal stuff for kicks."

"Steal stuff?"

Peter hung his head a little. "Yeah, they have shoplifting contests. They all hit a store, and whoever comes out with the most stuff, wins."

"Let me guess," Jake said. "If you come out with nothing, you get called 'wuss.'"

Peter hesitated, shrugged. "Basically, yes."

Jake took some time choosing his next words. "And what does the winner win, besides a police record that will keep him from getting a decent job when he *wants* to earn money, or from getting into the college he wants?" He said this while pulling abreast of Peter and staring at him until Peter was forced to look him in the eye. In Peter's family, Jake knew, getting into college was a big deal. They talked about it like it was going to happen tomorrow instead of several years away.

"I know, Jake. I know it's dumb."

Jake spoke more gently. "The guys won't really dump you if you refuse to lift stuff, will they? Or if they do, that's just the way it is, right, Peter?"

"Strange thing is," Peter responded, "the first few times I did it, I hated doing it." He pedaled more slowly. "Now I'm doing it sometimes without even thinking. I don't even need the stuff." His eyes found Jake's, and they seemed to be pleading.

"And?" Jake didn't want to push his buddy too hard.

"Ron's right. I'm going to get in bad trouble if I don't stop." He said this with a hardened face, looking away from Jake.

Jake switched to a warmer tone. "I just want to say that I know you're better than that."

Peter's eyes turned to meet his with what struck Jake as a flicker of gratitude, and a smile crept back to his face. Then he looked back up the slope above them and pointed to a plateau.

"Race you to that overlook."

The Peter Jake knew was back. Jake stood on his pedals and sprinted beside him, snorting as trail dust rose around them. Peter had a head start, but Jake was determined not to let him get away. They reached the plateau neck and neck, all but crashing into Ron, who was poised like the head stallion on a nearby rock overhang.

"Up to your usual, I see," Ron mused, backing away from the edge. "And before you start arguing, I've declared it a tie."

The three swung their bikes around and back onto the trail. They carried on in silence till Jake felt his thigh muscles burning. He was glad for the light-weight hiking boots Ron had urged them to wear instead of the runners in which they usually rode. As they gained elevation and dusk fell, he was surprised how cool the air became. They stopped to pull thermal tops from their packs and swallow the last drops from their water bottles, then run water from the nearby stream through their filter pump and refill the bottles.

As Jake had feared, Ron was now navigating by the stars and the clearest crescent moon Jake had ever seen. It looked close enough to reach out and touch. They must be getting close, Jake guessed, if only because the thin air was making him breathe harder. Even with the moonlight, his headlamp felt inadequate in the dark forest.

"It's just around the corner," Ron spoke up.

The corner turned out to be several corners, but sure enough, they soon stumbled upon camp: two pup tents and a stove all set up to make soup. Ron even fished some fresh-made cornbread out of his pack to serve with the soup, which had hardly settled in their stomachs before they unzipped their tent, crawled into their sleeping bags, and slept the deep sleep that only truly spent athletes can enjoy.

4   Trail-blazing

From the moment Peter opened his eyes and rolled out of his sleeping bag the next morning, all the way to the first break Ron allowed them at noon, one thought occupied his mind: finding a chance to ride some of the awesome terrain around them. Jake might be here for the money, but Peter was here for the adventure. The long slog up steep trails last night, never mind the indignity of being awakened by Ron's boot through the walls of the pup tent at seven o'clock this morning, had intensified his appetite for some great downhilling.

"One hour off at noon," Ron had pronounced after breakfast while revealing the tools they'd be working with: hatchets, wood saws, shovels, and an ax.

"No chainsaws?" Peter had asked, eyeing the state of the overgrown deer path they were to open into a bike trail.

"Nah, if it's that serious, we detour round it," the boss had said. "Anyhow, too dry up here to risk letting sparks fly. And we're not building a full-blown bike trail, just slightly extending and widening some disused hiking trails."

Good thing, Peter had thought, as he'd mopped his brow. But he'd also wondered, just for a second, if the lack of a chainsaw also had to do with noise level. Ron seemed overly concerned for someone with a license to build a bike trail about how much noise they were making.

"If we see backpackers, let me do the talking," he'd told them. "Not everyone thinks it's politically correct to build a bike trail through a provincial park, approved or not."

Approved or not, Peter mused. Was there a chance this wasn't all as approved as Ron had made it out to be?

Now it was quarter to twelve and Peter, unlike Ron and Jake, was checking his watch more frequently than he was swinging his ax in this heat. Jake and Ron, meanwhile, were not only working like dervishes, they were talking up a storm, laughing and going over Sam's Adventure Tours stories and gossip like they'd grown up together or something. Peter felt left out.

"Peter, grab the shovel and pack the ground up around that big exposed tree root," Ron finally addressed him. "Jake, thanks for clearing that brush out. How about taking the hatchet to the lower branches of that little tree?"

Peter ran his forearm over his sopping forehead and picked up the shovel. *Slave-driver. What is it Jake sees in that loser, anyway? You'd think the two of them were long-lost buddies, the way they act around each other.* Fifteen minutes later, pleased with having eliminated the roots, Peter glanced at his watch, dropped the shovel with a clatter, and inserted a dirty finger and thumb into his mouth to whistle loudly.

Ron and Jake lifted their heads, glanced at their watches, smiled, and wheeled their bikes behind Peter's back up the trail they'd cleared all morning, until they reached camp.

"Good progress," Ron declared as he set out some food and collapsed into a hammock he'd strung between two trees.

Peter slapped together the fastest peanut butter and jelly sandwich he'd ever tasted, and ingested a banana like it was liquid. Then, catching Jake's bemused face, he strapped on his helmet, hopped on his bike, and said, "See you at one o'clock."

He'd have waited for Jake, but he knew with one glance at his buddy's sagging shoulders that Jake wasn't going to be into it. Jake wanted food, rest, and probably a chance to hang with Ron without Peter around. And Peter craved time away from them. Those two were in together way too thick for his liking. He and Jake could do stuff together this evening, and the next day's lunch break. For now, this hard-earned trail was all Peter's, and, after the morning's sweat, he knew every rock, root, and turn on it.

Peter's hands gripped the handlebars as he picked up speed. He switched gears and tucked his head to go faster. Roots coiled like cobras, sharp rocks plotted to puncture his tires, and loose gravel lurked in corners waiting to make him skid out. He leaped or dodged all of these with ease, pouring on speed with a smile. Where the path bottomed out like the trough of a wave, he let his knees act as shock absorbers. He pretended to be a bike racer; he'd been reading up on their strategies on his favorite free-ride website.

Where the dirt path crested and moved along a ridge, he slowed to breathe deeply of the fresh air and appreciate the breeze and panorama. Mountaintops marched in every direction for hundreds of miles under a cloudless blue sky. One row of black crags behind him looked like his Grandpa's dentures except for the color, while some rusty-colored ridges with lots of loose gravel wore dog collars of boulders ready to roll on a moment's notice. He looked left and right at forested mountains rising so high the trees stopped abruptly before their rounded tops, making them resemble balding men. On the highest peaks, he noticed crusty snow defying the summer heat. These squeezed trickles of water that turned patches of grass below a bright green. As he swung his head around, he noted some caves peering out like deep eye sockets, and bulges of rock resembling bent, reddened noses. Elsewhere, pillars of lava mimicked petrified toothpaste, the kind that comes out in colorful stripes.

Peter shook his head in awe. What a sight. Like a bunch of cathedrals built where only clouds and mountain goats wander.

There was no time to take it all in. Not on a brief lunch hour. He pushed forward, reveling in the freedom, excitement, and beauty of the ride. How fast a path could change! One moment, steep and boulder-strewn; the next, flat and terrifying as slopes on both sides plunged to hidden valleys below. Then he was back into the trees, where branches the crew had missed this morning occasionally brushed his face and tree roots demanded that he keep his eyes trained on the path immediately ahead.

Never had he seen such varied terrain. From hard rock to soft dirt to scree slopes that seemed to drop away for miles. As he edged along one of these football fields of rock, he heard whistles. He paused and looked about. There it was again, shrill as those obnoxious whistles handed out as party favors. Wasn't he alone up here?

He peered about, waited until a whistle sounded again. There! He stared at the pile of rocks from which it had come and spotted a small creature bounding from one rock to another. Much bigger than a squirrel and amazingly vocal. The creature whistled again, echoed by others in the rocks. Another appeared, popping in and out of cavities in a way that reminded Peter of those silly hamsters in the arcade games where you're supposed to whack them with a hammer before they're gone. Hmmm, bet these creatures wouldn't think much of that game. He whistled back, making one of the creatures cock its head. It looked like a cross between a rabbit and a prairie dog, he decided. It was so appealing, he'd have loved to pick it up and pet it like he would a fat guinea pig. But these were wild, which was even better. Pikas! That's what they're called. He was glad he'd remembered. This mountain was alive with them! He was anything but alone, and that delighted him, somehow.

"Hey, pikas!" he shouted, following that with whistling. "See ya around!" And he hopped back on his bike and spun around toward camp, excited to tell Ron and Jake about his find.

That afternoon, they cleared an amazing amount

of trail. Peter felt stoked by the fresh mountain air, and the deer, sheep, birds, and other wildlife they kept seeing. He was proud of what the combined brawn of three fit guys could do. He felt more a part of the team than he had in the morning.

But something nagged at him, something about Ron's behavior. Their leader seemed too evasive about his plans and kind of jumpy up here. Peter would have liked to speculate about his uneasy feelings with Jake, but he knew his friend was over-trusting of, and over-loyal to, Ron. And Peter had nothing to go on but an elusive gut feeling. Jake would just interpret that as jealousy. On the positive side, Peter thought, at least Ron had no access to beer up here. So Peter shrugged off his unsettled feeling and let the sunshine evaporate any negativity.

That allowed his overall good mood to carry right through to the next morning, when he awoke with an idea. He incubated it until he decided Ron was in a good mood, half an hour after they'd finished breakfast and started working on the trail.

"Hey, Ron. If we clear a phenomenal amount of trail tomorrow, could we win a few hours off to build dirt jumps somewhere with some soft dirt? Then we could do tricks and stuff. I've seen a couple of places that might work for that."

Ron straightened his back from dragging away

some branches and turned his shirtless, sweat-drenched body toward Peter. "We're not here for fun …" he began in a hard voice, but to Peter's surprise, Jake broke in.

"But just a tiny bit of fun would make us work really, really hard both sides of that break, don't you think? We could guarantee you it'll be worth it."

Nicely said, Peter thought. Just the right suck-up tone, and Ron always listens to you. Sure enough, their leader cracked a smile.

"A guarantee, eh? So if I mark a spot tomorrow that I don't think you can possibly reach by three o'clock, and you do, we can knock off at three. And if you have the energy to shovel dirt into piles at that point, I'll eat my hat." He grabbed his soiled baseball cap, which dislodged the ponytail shoved through it, and pretended to chew on it.

Jake and Peter laughed. "It's a deal!"

They worked hard all morning and afternoon, as if training for the next day's feat, and rushed to make dinner while Ron chopped some wood. After a quiet evening, during which all three read books by Ron's lantern while taking turns feeding the campfire, Peter and Jake volunteered to turn in early.

"If I didn't know you had nowhere to go, I'd think you were up to something," Ron teased, but he nodded as they said goodnight and piled into their tent.

"We can do it tomorrow, you know," Peter whispered to Jake as they zipped themselves into their bags and watched their guide shovel dirt onto the campfire to put it out.

"Of course we can," Jake agreed.

The next morning, true to his word, Ron hiked well past their trail building's furthest point, the boys at his heels, and hung a piece of pink plastic tape on a tree impossibly far from where they'd laid down their tools the night before.

"That piece of tape is quittin' time," he declared, face stern but eyes soft.

"We're on it!" Peter promised as the three returned to their worksite. He and Jake shoveled, hacked, tore, and toted obstacles like an ironman duo. Ron worked alongside them, hardly uttering a word all day, just issuing the occasional reminder to drink water in this heat so as not to get dehydrated. The boys opted for a fifteen-minute lunch hour, during which Ron seemed in unusually good humor.

"So, Ron, did you always dream of running your own adventure travel company?" Peter ventured.

Ron, who'd pulled his cap over his face as he lay in some shade, mumbled from beneath it, "Who, me?

Not likely. I'm never in one place long enough to run anything."

"But this is a big venture for you, and it looks like you're expecting it to go big."

Ron moved grimy fingers to his cap and lifted it just long enough to apply a sideways glance at Peter.

"Nah, just long enough to make a buck, then I'll be onto somethin' else. Who knows what or where, so long as I get back to Keremeos regularly."

"Make a quick buck?" Peter pressed. "No one ever makes a quick buck from a small business. There won't be any money in this for years, so you have to stick with it. Unless you know something I don't," he added boldly.

Ron was sitting up now, his face a study in temper control. He was silent for what seemed ages, then cleared his throat as if about to speak. Then he was silent again as he fiddled with his baseball cap in his hands. Finally, he glanced about the forest as if the trees might be spies and spoke, eyes on a patch of dry grass.

"It's not me who has the business, actually," he began. "Two guys I went to high school with have the business. I'm just the trail builder. They hired me to make it real quick this summer. They're paying me good to do it, so it *is* a quick buck."

He lifted his eyes and looked the boys over. "Sorry

I kind of twisted the truth a bit to get you out here."

"But why wouldn't we have come if you'd said you were just building a trail for someone else's operation?" Peter asked, even more perplexed.

"Guess I didn't want your parents asking lots of questions. Was hoping to get you guys on board fast," Ron replied, looking away and twisting his cap into an even tighter wad.

"Something else I should mention," he continued. "Paperwork on the license isn't totally through, so we could get hassled if we meet people. That's why I'm always trying to keep us from making too much of a racket. And if we meet up with anyone, as I said, leave them to me."

"Lots of parks have illegal bike trails," Peter observed. "Officials can't keep up with bikers, and some regions don't even care. We'd have come even if we knew the license wasn't all the way through, wouldn't we, Jake? It's not like we haven't helped construct trails on the sly before."

Peter glanced at Jake, who seemed to be tensed up and unwilling to answer.

"It's true that some park administrators turn a blind eye till someone gets hurt," Ron agreed as he lay back against a dirt pile and pulled his cap over his eyes again. "But my friends have a license for commercial bike touring here. Ninety percent through."

"But can you trust these guys you're working for, Ron?" Peter knew the second he'd said it that he shouldn't have. If Ron was in a good mood, you could question him a little, but you had to keep an eye on him like you'd keep an eye on a cat. One minute he'd be relaxed and open to play, and the next, his paw would strike out, sometimes without claws retracted. Then, leave him alone again for a few minutes, and he might be mellow again.

"I said they were high school mates," he shouted, eyes flashing. "Guys I've known for more years than you two have been alive."

The boys were quiet.

"Okay, one was a good friend in high school. Name of Hank. I trust him. The other, Laszlo, is a nasty piece of work, and I'd just as soon Hank didn't hang out with him. Laszlo is the kind of guy who brings out the worst in other people. Scares them. Bullies them. But he doesn't scare me."

Ron's voice was calmer now, and he was picking up pebbles absent-mindedly and placing them in little piles. Smooth pebbles in one pile, and sharp rocks in another, Peter noticed.

"Anyway, Hank told me they'd gone into business together with this bike trail permit thing, and they needed someone to coordinate the building of it. I needed work — Sam's Adventure Tours doesn't have enough work for me this year. And Hank and I go way back, and I liked the idea of helpin' him out. He was my best friend way back, even though we've kinda been out of touch. I know he's been livin' rough the last few years, so it's good to see he's got himself a job, even if it is with Laszlo. And I know a thing or two about building bike trails."

Peter noticed a point of pride in Ron's voice. He figured Hank and Laszlo were lucky to have brought on a hard laborer like Ron. No one could outwork the man when he was sober, that was for sure. And he and Jake had been admiring Ron's riding skills all the way up the trail.

"Ron, did you grow up in Keremeos?" That was Jake's voice. It dawned on Peter that Jake had been silent a long time. Peter didn't mind that his buddy was taking up a safer line of questioning.

"Yup."

"Still have family around?"

This prompted Ron to sit up, remove his cap, and turn to Jake. "Just a sister." Peter noticed his facial features grow unusually soft and open. "She's the reason I'm back in Keremeos."

The boys were quiet, waiting to see what else he'd say.

"I'm helpin' her pay off her mortgage. Her no-good dirtbag scum of a husband took off on her, leavin' her with a new baby, and she otherwise stands to lose the house, not that it's much of a house, but it's somethin'." He leveled his gaze at them, and Peter noticed, not for the first time, how incredibly blue his eyes were. He also decided Ron had uttered more words the last few minutes than he'd ever spilled in front of Jake and Peter in all the months they'd known him.

"The house you're in?" he asked.

"Nah, hers is smaller, a block away, and I'm giving up my rental next month to move into hers."

"Mmm," Peter said distractedly, still chewing on the fact that Ron hadn't been straight with them about the bike touring business and the trail permit.

What else was he hiding? Did his friends really have a license on the brink of coming through, or were they and Ron using the boys to build an illegal trail? Just because Ron had lectured Peter on stealing and police records didn't mean Ron himself was squeaky clean, Peter suddenly thought. Or maybe Ron's friends were using Ron and Ron didn't know it, which wouldn't be that big a deal, except why would they pay big money for his trail-building?

"What about your mom or dad? Did they move away?" Jake was asking, softly, with a flicker of hesitation.

Peter started when Ron leaped up, grabbed a shovel,

and walked a few paces away. Then he paused, and without turning, said, "My dad disappeared on us when I was your age, boys, then my mom died. I looked after my sister awhile, then took off, learned to fend for myself. Been all over the world, done a ton of things. Survival is a good thing to learn, even if you never have occasion to use it."

Peter, watching Jake out of the corner of his eye, wasn't surprised to see his friend's sudden change of expression. He was clearly startled, and fascinated. What else would he be? So Ron's dad had done a disappearing act, just like Jake's father. Peter remembered that Ron had guided for an adventure tour company in South America before he'd worked for Sam's Adventure Tours. He'd always been one tough dude, though not much of a communicator. But maybe he was okay, really.

As Ron rammed his shovel into some dirt, the boys scrambled up, knowing that social time was over. Whatever else Ron was, Peter decided as the three got back to their duties, he was impossible to outwork. He was super strong and took breaks so rarely that Peter hardly dared slack off more than a few minutes every hour. Yet today, of course, Peter and Jake had plenty of incentive not to sit down. They were working their way toward that magic piece of pink tape. Peter kept checking his watch. One o'clock. Two o'clock. Two-fifteen. At two-thirty, Peter dropped his tools and sprinted ahead to check how close they were. He burst back into their clearing with the news: "Pink tape up ahead! We can do it, old buddy. Don't stop now."

Ron offered no reaction, just kept shoveling.

When they reached the tape, the boys emitted cheers that sent a flock of birds flapping from the branches above. They grabbed some cookies from their backpacks, downed so much water that their bellies gurgled, and placed their hands on their hips as they surveyed a nearby clearing.

"So, dirt is pretty loose here," Peter declared. "What do you say we build a jump here? With three of us, it'll go fast."

"Who says I'm in on this?" Ron retorted, leaning on his shovel handle. "I'll just watch you for a minute, and maybe work on the trail ahead while yer playin'. Don't go playin' so hard that you can't pull full weight tomorrow, or you'll get no such lucky break again."

"Suit yourself," Peter said brazenly, realizing that he'd never normally say anything cheeky to Ron, except that Ron seemed to be unusually friendly today.

Within two hours, the boys had two five-foot-high piles of dirt creating a cool, eight-foot gap. They stamped the dirt piles down between, adding to their height, singing and yahooing as they went.

"Looks like a pair of fangs rising out of the ground," Peter observed.

"Fangs that can bite," Jake returned.

As they started the transition landing, they were surprised to see Ron emerge from the trail ahead. "Pathetic," he joked. "That all you can do in two hours? You obviously need more muscle here. Dare you to keep up with me." With that, he went into a high-speed shoveling mode that they scrambled to try to match. They couldn't come anywhere near equaling his shovel rate, of course, which only seemed to spur the man on. When the run-out was finished, Ron stepped back, clapped his hands free of dirt, and sat down cross-legged, leaning against a tree a short distance away.

"Okay, kids, I'm ready for my show. And it better be good, 'cause I paid good for it."

Peter went first, of course. "Let me show you two how this is done!" he declared as he pushed his bike uphill above the jump, swung a leg over and hesitated. He stood on his pedals, brow knotted with intensity, and decided he could get more than enough speed to clear the gap. He left the ground with focused ferocity, but as his rear wheel went skyward and his front wheel dipped, he cursed with frustration.

"Whoooooooooaaa!" he shouted angrily as he overshot the jump and his tire hit the ground with a thud well past the transition. He felt himself flung to the ground. As dust settled around him, however, he began laughing and rubbing his dirt-caked face.

"Guess I hit it with too much speed."

"That's how you do it, is it?" Jake offered with a belly laugh, echoed by Ron's chuckling. "Thanks for the clinic."

Peter drew himself up a little sheepishly and gestured like a television host introducing a special guest as he said loudly, "Next up, folks, is the one and only Jake Evans to show us how to really do it."

Peter backed up, sat down beside Ron, and watched Jake take a couple of tentative pumps at the pedals, then coast in, readying himself for liftoff. He squinted as Jake's front wheel cleared the transition, then smirked as his buddy "cased" his rear wheel hard, hooking it on top of the fresh pile of earth. Good thing Jake's bike had enough suspension to suck up the bang, he thought, as he watched his partner roll slowly down the "trannie," or transition.

Peter jumped up, happy to take his turn again. Ron crossed his arms as he lay back with a grin and continued to take it all in. Over the next twenty minutes, as Peter and Jake gained confidence, both began hitting the transition more and more consistently. Peter didn't mind that Jake was the first to try pulling a hand off the bars in mid-air, because Peter was first to twist his bike slightly, by turning his bars and shifting his hips to the left, showing the modest beginnings of a "tabletop" move. He felt in control, which made him puff with pride.

"That's enough for me!" he admitted after dismounting and collapsing onto the ground panting.

"Me too," Jake agreed.

"Want to see an X-up?" Ron's voice suddenly boomed out.

Peter and Jake both started to shake their heads no, until Peter realized Ron had said "see," not "do." Peter turned, smiled, and nodded vigorously as Ron winked, mounted his bike, and passed the boys, heading for their starting point.

Churning his pedals at breakneck speed, the big man went for the first dirt pile. Up and over he shot, then floated above the forest floor. Like a mariner cranking on a ship's wheel, he twisted his handlebars and front wheel half a rotation, forcing his arms to cross at the elbows, before quickly rotating them back in time for the landing.

Whomp! The bike rolled neatly down the fresh-built mound, Ron grinning wider than Peter had ever seen a grown man grin. He dropped his bike and strolled over to the boys, who collapsed with him onto the softness of the second dirt pile, like kids jumping into a leaf pile.

After a moment of quiet, Jake spoke in a slightly timid voice. "Ron, did your dad just disappear and never write again?"

Ron, face lifted to the sun, didn't answer right away. He kept fingering one of his earrings. In fact, Peter had just decided he wasn't going to reply when a soft, bass voice rose from the heap. "I know where he is, Jake. But doesn't do any of us any good. He's behind bars, and he never wrote after my mom died. That's as good as disappeared. I won't let my nephew grow up poor and without a man in his life, though. I'm gonna do my part. That's why we're building this trail."

With that, he rose in one motion, stalked to his bike without a backward glance, and rode away, calf muscles swiftly bringing the bike to life.

5   Crash

Day Four dawned as clear and warm as all the others had been. Even though Peter's body had adjusted to the rigors of hacking at roots and shoveling from sunup to sundown — and he was proud of the distance they'd advanced in just a few days — he craved more sleep. Their routine, now well established, was grating on him. Every morning at seven o'clock, Ron would kick them out of bed. They'd eat breakfast as chipmunks and squirrels scampered about their feet and birds swooped down to alight on their shoulders if they placed a crumb there. Occasionally, mule deer accompanied by spotted fawns would wander into the clearing, their dark, oversized ears flicking. Almond-shaped eyes would watch the campers as they made lunch sandwiches and hopped onto their bikes. Then Ron and the boys would commute to the day's worksite and put in grueling hours until suppertime. Each evening, too, the three took turns making supper, usually freeze-dried soup or pasta with the occasional treat of canned meat.

This morning it was Peter's turn to make breakfast, and he'd foolishly offered to make French toast. French toast? Had he been out of his mind? He'd never cooked before in his life. No need to in his house. Jake, self-appointed world's expert on cooking, had explained everything to him the night before. Eggs, milk, and bread. Soak 'em, them slop 'em into the frying pan with some cooking oil. How hard could that be? But so far, he'd burned three slices, and Jake and Ron were making it worse by not saying a thing. Not only were they not stepping in to help, but they were smirking and chuckling behind his back. Those two were way too friendly. Employees shouldn't get buddy-buddy with their bosses, ever. Especially when their bosses are friendly one moment and explosive as dynamite the next. Just because Ron had been easygoing for a day or two — well, easygoing for Ron, which wasn't saying much — didn't mean Peter was taking a liking to him. Despite his good intentions toward his sister, he was a drifter; hadn't he said as much himself? But he and Jake could cook, and Peter couldn't, and there was no good pretending otherwise.

"Come on guys, help me out a little. Otherwise we won't have any egg and milk stuff left," Peter said, pride smarting to say that much.

"Nope, you get another try. Just put more oil in and keep the heat lower," Ron said as he moved food supplies around in the little chicken-wire box that kept small animals from invading their stock.

Peter sighed, scraped black guck out of the pan, and plopped oil in again. He mixed up some more milk from their powdered supply in a separate pan, sprinkled in more of the gross yellow powder from the dried egg packet, and poked limp pieces of bread around in the liquid. Then he grabbed the spatula, to which blackened bits still clung, and lifted the dripping pieces of bread into the frying pan, this time applying as much attention to the browning French toast as he would to a biking DVD.

"Done!" he pronounced proudly as they achieved golden-brown status and Jake and Ron pressed around him with plates.

"A-1 job, sir. We'll make a camp cook of you yet," Ron declared, smothering his helping with syrup before passing the bottle around. "This'll stoke us up for the day ahead. No pausing by that jump on the way, you know. It's history now, till evening, anyway."

At least the person who makes breakfast doesn't have to do dishes, Peter reflected, as he trotted down to the nearby creek to run water through their water filter. He drank so much of the new supply he had to do another shift of filtering before tugging their freshly filled pots and bottles up the hill.

"Ah, and water boy too," Jake commented, as he emptied the dish suds over a boulder. "Ron, I think we can offer him a decent recommendation to future employers."

"Suck-up," Peter hissed out of Ron's earshot, enjoying the startled look that crossed Jake's face.

They rode the distance to the bike jump in silence. Though a little sore from yesterday's exertions, Peter wasn't about to show it. As they dropped their bikes and picked up their tools, he attacked the nearest set of exposed roots, shoveling dirt atop as best he could. He tried to picture a happy-go-lucky set of twenty tourists on their shiny new bikes playing follow-the-leader behind a guide. Wouldn't be fun guiding them, he decided. Probably a bunch of spoiled brats without a clue how to change a punctured tire, let alone do a jump. They'd complain about his cooking and grump about the cold or heat or wet. They'd expect him to fix or tune up their bikes every evening. They'd probably move agonizingly slowly. And their bikes weren't even full-suspension, he reminded himself smugly.

The morning passed relatively quickly, despite his stiff muscles. On the stroke of noon, they biked back to camp for lunch, he and Jake passing the jump with longing glances. Sometimes they ate sandwiches at the worksite, but today they'd voted to return to camp to open a can of soup. As fast as he could down his soup and sandwich, Peter said, "Well, guys, I'm outta here. See ya at one! Catch me if you can!"

He knew they wouldn't follow. They were already engaged in their buddy-buddy chatter. They were probably enjoying the chance to rest. Fine for them, but Peter was a man of action, and lunch hours were what he lived for now. As he reached their jump, he threw in a few tricks for good measure. Not that anyone was watching, so what was the point? He had exploring in mind, wanted to see what else this trail might get up to.

In no time at all, it seemed, he had reached the stopping point of their path-clearing operation. That meant he should turn around, not knowing what the overgrown animal trail had in store from here. But he had at least half an hour before he had to head back, and what the heck, he had to tackle it after the lunch break one way or another. He'd just slow down a bit and do a short exploratory.

As it turned out, the path — relatively obstruction-free for now — wound downhill at a leisurely, safe pitch. These deer are smart, Peter thought; they take sensible routes and zigzag sharply back and forth where the terrain dictates a traverse. As the steepness increased and his body began vibrating, he wondered where exactly Ron's trailblazing was leading and made a mental note to ask him to show them on his professional-looking contour maps. As his teeth began rattling, he wondered why Ron was refusing to hire them as guides when his operation was up and running. Not that Peter wanted to. Well, maybe he did. It would be interesting, and anyway, money was money. As he lifted up on his handlebars just in time to jump a log across the trail, he wondered why Jake so trusted and liked the moody outdoorsman.

Trust was not something Peter could easily award their ponytailed host. Even if Ron had his good days, something about the man didn't sit well with Peter, though Jake was generally more reliable on matters of instinct. Trust was something he had in this bike, however. The way it took these curves, held its grip on the slippery gravel patches, was impressive. He'd never be able to reach such speeds on his bicycle at home, not on crazy ground like this. The trees around him were becoming a green blur; the path was dropping at dizzying speed now. Maybe the deer had cut this portion while being chased by a cougar, he thought, laughing aloud as he lurched with the trail around a sharp corner.

The laughing stopped abruptly as his trusty steed

tripped over an exposed root and bucked him off. Fear electrified his joints as he felt himself flying through the air. There wasn't time to think or tuck up into a position that might minimize the damage. He saw the rocky slope coming at him and regretted for that split second that he wasn't wearing body armor.

Then the surface hit him hard, rock hard, nearly smacking him senseless. He lay still, conscious of being conscious, but his breath totally knocked out of him. As he struggled to breathe, pain sensors from altogether too many points of his body began checking in with his brain.

"Oh man," he groaned, closing his eyes.

6   The Chunnel Theory

Jake knew when his watch hit one o'clock that something had happened. He had a sense about these things, but he also knew Peter would never have risked Ron's wrath by showing up late. He wasn't surprised somehow when, on the stroke of one, Ron jumped out of his hammock and grabbed a first-aid kit from his jumble of gear to stuff in his pack.

"Come on, kid," he growled as he hopped on his bike and took off down the path.

They could see Peter's tire tracks in the soft dirt, could tell he'd been speeding by where he'd taken the banked turns, could identify the log he'd jumped. When they reached their morning's finish point, they exchanged knowing glances and carried on, cautiously. When they found his bike in a heap just beyond where a pothole met a knotty tree root, they braked and peered down an exposed scree slope. And there, to Jake's consternation, was a bloodied Peter curled up as if in pain, on a flat rock in the middle of a sea of sharp, broken-up rocks. He was also just feet away from a family of shaggy, hump-shouldered mountain goats. The goats turned their long faces and pointy black horns to the newcomers and raised black eyes, noses, and lips to check them out. The downy kid wobbled on legs as spindly as Jake's felt.

"Peter?" Jake called out, startling the handsome creatures, who bounded off, beards wagging, bony backsides bobbing. At any other time, Jake would have thought this wildlife sighting a treat, would've pulled a camera out to try and record the cute baby and its family. But he was more interested in the fact that Peter's head had turned toward them.

"Sorry I'm late," Peter commented dryly. "I don't think I've broken anything, but I wasn't absolutely sure if I could or should climb back up to the trail. Then these goats distracted me. Hated to scare them away."

Ron, Jake figured, could have lost it right there, could have lectured Peter about safety and reckless use of borrowed equipment. Could have harped about how he was already pressed to finish this trail by his deadline. Instead, he climbed down and set to work checking Peter over. Like a patient medic, he lifted and probed each limb.

"Does this hurt? Can you move that? Did you black out at all?"

He produced alcohol wipes and sterile pads from his first-aid kit and touched them to the largest wounds, eyes on Peter's face, gentle as a father. Peter winced once or twice, but as far as Jake could tell, none were still bleeding freely. All were just ugly surface gashes, some with small stones embedded until Ron coaxed them out.

One by one, Peter helping, Ron dressed the serious gashes and cleaned the rest. After a while, he helped Peter to his feet and dug into his pack for a clean T-shirt, which he drenched with the contents of his water bottle.

"Jake, help clean the rest of the dried blood off," he suggested.

"It's okay, Jake. I can do that," Peter offered.

With steady leaps, Ron scrambled back up the slope to Peter's bike. "Bike's okay, in better shape than you," he shouted. "You're takin' the rest of the day off, if you promise not to get blood on my hammock or eat us out of camp. There'll be overtime due when you recover," he added sternly.

Jake couldn't believe it. Ron was being really decent, considering what Peter deserved. Jake was impressed. He felt a warm rush of gratitude, a sense that he and Peter were in good hands in an unfamiliar wilderness.

They lost a lot of work time walking Peter back to camp before returning to their tools. Though Jake and Ron made good progress that afternoon considering they'd lost one set of hands, Jake sensed that the slowdown was eating at Ron.

"Bet he's good for a full day's work by tomorrow," Jake ventured.

"I reckon so, though he'll be stiff," Ron agreed.

"So where's this trail going to end up, Ron?"

Ron's head lifted and he seemed to hesitate.

"Down this slope and up the next, then down and up a few more," he replied at length with a twinkle in his eye.

"Seems like we're basically heading south," Jake dared to press further. "We must be near the border."

"Not very," Ron answered, eyes on his work. An awkward silence hung between them as they hacked branches, hauled rocks, and smoothed bumps.

"Peter's grandparents live straight south of here, in Winthrop," Jake prattled on, trying to draw Ron back into the cheerful mood he'd been in over lunch. "He was leader of the first crew of smokejumpers in the United States, if you can believe Peter. Ever heard of smokejumpers?"

"Used to work the fire lines myself," Ron replied, stripping off his shirt and straining against a large rock in the center of their path. His muscles glistened in the sun. "Makes this work feel like a holiday."

"Speaking of holidays, when exactly will the bike tours start up, and is there any chance Peter and I can apply to your friends to be guides?" Jake asked boldly. He knew Peter had asked and been turned down already, but he'd decided to try anyway.

Ron rose, pulled the rubber band off his sweat-soaked ponytail, yanked his hair back into place, and snapped the holder back on, all the while staring down the path.

"You're too young and that's the all of it," he finally said. "But I appreciate your last-minute help here. Has to be finished in six days, on Monday, and the two crewmen who were helping me till now, I had to fire for slacking off on the job and sneakin', uh, party substances along."

"You mean drugs."

"Stuff that put 'em in no frame of mind to be helping me safely or cooperatively. Then I got the wild notion that you and Peter might be available. And you're both steady workers, doing me proud even if Peter's lunch hours need to be supervised from now on." He cracked a smile and turned his stubbly chin toward Jake.

Jake smiled. "He's learned his lesson, and I'll stick with him on his hours off." They worked in silence for a while longer. "Ron?"

"Yes, kid."

"Even if the three of us worked all-out for two weeks, I don't see how we're going to get from the western to the eastern borders of the park, if that's where we're heading. And I didn't notice any roads on the park's eastern border when I looked at a map before we left Chilliwack, just a creek. Is there access and a parking lot there or something? Is that where these tours will end?"

Ron, smile returning, rested his chin on his shovel and mopped his face. "Okay, here's how it hangs. Another crew is workin' from the other direction, and we're going to meet up in the middle, neat as you please, on Monday. Just like the way the Chunnel was built."

"The Chunnel?"

"The English Channel tunnel between England and France."

"Oh, yeah. Well, why didn't you tell us?" Jake said, beaming as he applied his ax to a thin tree branch otherwise perfectly positioned to behead a passing cyclist. "That's brilliant."

Brilliant, he decided, was also a perfect description for the butterfly that alighted on a rock near Jake's foot just then. Dropping his ax, Jake cupped his hands around the wings.

"Ron, can you grab that jar and little box out of

my backpack for me? Got some business to do for my little sister." Jake felt his face redden a little. Ron just smiled, unzipped the pack for him, even unscrewed the jar's lid so that he could pop the butterfly in.

Ron raised his eyebrows as Jake produced cotton balls and a tiny bottle of rubbing alcohol from inside the big jar. Jake soaked the little balls in alcohol before dropping them into the jar beside the butterfly just like Alyson had told him to do. He even remembered to reach in and pinch the butterfly's thorax to stun it before screwing the lid back on, so it wouldn't damage its wings before it succumbed to the gassing. Later, he'd lift the specimen out and place it on the special card inside the little box, its wings folded neatly down and body tucked into a speacil indent.

"What an organized kid you are. And got three good-lookin' ones in there already. Lucky kid sister." Ron laughed, but it was a kind laugh, as if he understood about sisters and promises.

The two worked until both had brought up the topic of supper one too many times. Leaving their tools where they lay, trusting they'd be safe overnight, they hopped on their bikes and headed back to camp.

"Hey, what tricks can you do on your bike that you haven't shown me on the dirt piles already?"

"Not many. Never had a full-suspension bike before,"

Jake admitted. He didn't want to add that he couldn't afford repairs to his hard-tail very often, either.

"Do me a nose manual, at least. Trail dips ahead."

Jake smiled, pedaled hard, and as his bike shot down the slope, leaned forward and squeezed his front brake. He felt his rear tire rise off the ground and managed to maintain control as he carried on down the hill riding on his front wheel only. After he'd set down and let Ron catch up, he heard his boss shout, "Okay, go back up the hill, come down aiming at the same lip, and do a one-hander this time."

As if I wouldn't be able to do that, Jake thought. He cycled back up, whirled around, and sped toward the uneven piece of ground to get a bit of air. As soon as he was up, he took one hand off his handlebars, even daringly moved it all the way to one side like an extended wing, before returning it for the landing.

"Nah, a suicide one-hander," Ron egged him on. Jake wiped a sweaty hand on his trousers and made his way back up the hill. Down he came at the now familiar lip, cleared it, and swung an arm all the way to his back for a split second. He barely managed to return it in time to land. Phew, that was close. Ron had better not ask me to do a no-hander, he thought.

"Alright, kid! You're happening!"

Jake grinned and ducked as Ron reached out to pat the top of his helmet fondly.

"Okay, let's hit it up the rest of the way back to camp," Ron said, tugging on the ponytail sticking out from under his helmet.

Jake followed, shredding slopes and landing little drops right behind the guide, who made it all look much easier than it was. When they tired of vigorous feats, they rode side by side wherever the trail allowed, laughing and joking most of the rest of the way.

Jake surveyed the warm sunset and the way snow collars around nearby peaks formed smiles. Ever so vaguely, he recalled bike trips with his dad, back when life had been perfect. Back before his dad had disappeared and everything had fallen apart. Days like today, it seemed like life had put itself back together again. Days like today, he felt like he'd turned a corner, so to speak. And that's just what he was doing now at an impressive clip. Turning corners and hoping Peter had gotten just bored enough this afternoon to rustle them up some supper.

7   Eyes in the Forest

Peter was bored. Glad to be off duty, for sure, but definitely too sore to mount his bike and go somewhere. First he tried reading in the hammock, but visits from whisky-jacks and chipmunks soon distracted him. He tried going for a walk, but his bruised body voted for an immediate retreat to the hammock. He fixed himself some chocolate milk, but that only made him more restless.

The first time twigs snapped on the forest floor nearby, he raised his eyes, mildly curious. Deer, he hoped. But this deer, if that's what it was, remained out of sight, no matter how motionless Peter tried to stay.

Wishing Ron had allowed them to bring handheld video games, binoculars, or cameras, Peter drummed his fingers on the cover of his book as it rested in his lap. Even a deck of cards would have been better than staring at the same old trees all afternoon. Solitaire sounded better than solitary.

The second time twigs cracked, he swung his head in that direction and stared, super alert. Again, he played the waiting game, and again, he grew bored waiting for his visitor's next move. Finally, tossing his book on the ground, he heaved his battered legs out of his perch and stood. Ouch. Might be a day or two before he'd be up to riding anything interesting. At least he hadn't broken anything. He stared at the two pup tents in their clearing, mentally sifting through everything he and Jake had brought on the trip. Nothing to entertain him but his paperback novel. He eyed Ron's tent, wondering what their guide had that might amuse him. Would Ron mind if he rummaged through his belongings? Ha! But how would he know? Peter turned away to lower his temptation, sighed, leaned over to pick his book up off the ground, and spotted a flat, shiny rock, which he picked up. Slowly, he eased his legs back up into the hammock, turning the rock over and over in his hands. No point riling up a moody boss more than he already had. Unpredictable fellow. Nice, then grumpy, then nice, then grumpy.

Snap. This time, the noise came from the forest behind his left shoulder. Peter turned, and his body tensed. Definitely something much larger than a chipmunk or bird. Was it the same thing that had been hanging around all the past hour, or was each twig that broke a sign of a new, invisible intruder? Easy to imagine things in the forest. He lifted his rock, aimed it in the direction of the last sounds, and let fly.

"Take that, you stupid deer," he shouted. He expected to hear the crashing of something's retreat, but he heard nothing. Even the birds and chipmunks had disappeared. The woods were eerily silent. *You won't see a cougar up here*, Peter had assured Jake on the ride up.

Peter shivered, even in the afternoon's heat, and opened his novel. He tried very, very hard to get drawn into it, must have read two full pages before he realized he wasn't taking in a single word. He was aware of only one sensation: that of being watched.

Something to eat. That was the answer. He'd fix himself another snack, maybe crumble some bread to coax a chipmunk or two back into the clearing to keep him company. Except that Ron had said not to feed the animals or they wouldn't gather and store what they needed to get through the winter. He glanced at his watch. Ron and Jake wouldn't be back for another few hours. What was he supposed to do to keep from going stir-crazy, sing or something?

Hey! Ron had a harmonica. That would be something to do. He could always tell Ron he'd needed to make noise to scare away wild animals. He limped over to Ron's tent, hesitated, looked about the woods again, then dived in. Gross. He wrinkled his nose. Stunk like a locker room in here. Crumpled sleeping bag, small lantern, filthy socks tossed in one corner of the tent, a small bag of clothing in another. A paperback novel. Peter reached for it, curious what type of trash Ron might read. Tacky secret-agent story, but at least the man can read, he thought. Peter spied a pocket hanging from the side seam of the tent, bulging with some small item. He stuck his fingers in; they closed around something small and metal, but it wasn't the right size for a harmonica. A flat, round tin. He opened it. Yuck. Chewing tobacco. No wonder Ron's teeth were yellow and his breath stank. He closed it and shoved it back into the pocket, which made a crinkly gum wrapper fall out. As he picked it up to replace it, he noticed "4907111. J.G. (José)" written in cramped scrawl on it.

Probably some woman had scribbled down her phone number and handed it to Ron in the last bar he'd visited. Peter returned the piece of paper to its place under the tobacco tin and crawled to the clothes bag. He dug a hand deep down into it, feeling for the little instrument. That's when he heard a fresh sound of branches moving nearby, followed by what resembled a soft padding of feet. Feet? Or paws? Retreating, ever so quietly.

Just then, his fingers closed around the harmonica. Fast as possible and shaking just a little, he wiped it as clean as he could with his shirt, brought it to his lips, and played a shaky tune. He didn't care if it was musical. He was going for loud. Loud and defiant. The kind that might scare a wild animal away. He backed out of the tent, still playing, and scanned every tree, shadow, and patch of ground in sight. He played for half an hour, until his lips were dry and his wristwatch said Jake and Ron would arrive in another hour. Then he buried the harmonica back in Ron's bag, made sure the tent looked exactly as it had when he'd entered it, and moved back to the hammock, this time with a kitchen knife in his hand. But the tension was gone. Birds twittered and chipmunks chased about camp, occasionally leaping atop a rock opposite the hammock and scolding Peter at high volume, their tails vibrating with the effort.

"Oh yeah? You think I'm lazy?" he addressed them. "I'll show you. I'm going for a walk."

With that, he stood up, jammed the knife in his back pocket, and limped slowly out of camp. He didn't follow any particular route, just ambled through the dry undergrowth randomly, avoiding anything that required climbing, scrambling, stepping over, or ducking under. He stopped frequently — to listen for sounds of being stalked, he told himself, but the truth was, after just fifteen minutes of walking, his bruised and battered body wanted no more exercise. As he sat down against a tree to gather energy for the return to camp, he gradually became aware of voices, distant enough that he could barely register them as voices, in the opposite direction to camp.

Hikers, he guessed. Seemed strange they hadn't run into hiking parties before now — although maybe it wasn't strange, given that they weren't near any of the park's designated hiking trails. They were, after all, forging their own routes well south of the park's main activity, keeping to little-used or abandoned hiking trails and animal paths. Happy to meet other people to talk to on this boring afternoon, he edged forward as quietly as he could, just for the fun of seeing if he could sneak up on them without being seen first. As he drew near, he began to hear snatches of their conversation.

"Colombia … shipment next week … nephews got a raw deal … little sneak."

Now he could make out two men, two sleeping bags hanging from a clothesline between trees, a small pile of gear, and a tiny cooking stove into which one of the men — a short, out-of-shape one — was pouring water into a pot. The other man was a giant: tall and powerful enough to look like a National Football League linebacker. Hey, this was Canada, so make that an enforcer on a National Hockey League team, Peter thought with a rueful smile as he paused, suddenly stricken with second thoughts about making himself known to the two.

He watched as the shorter man accidentally spilled the water he was pouring. Without warning, the bigger man cuffed him.

"You idiot. You put out the burner. Can't do anything right, can you?"

The shorter man cowered and mumbled apologies, dabbing a filthy towel around the burner to mop up the spill. As he turned to fetch more water, the giant raised his boot and shoved it into his backside, nearly sending him flying. Peter felt the blood drain from his face and his fists curl as he pulled carefully out of sight behind a tree. Why did the smaller man put up with that? What was going on here?

The men had stopped talking, making Peter wonder if they'd spotted him. He was trying to decide whether to step forward or retreat when the deepvoiced hulk spoke. His words sent a chill down Peter's spine.

"This is going to be the best damn smuggling operation in America's history, y'know. Just a couple of months of working this border and we'll be retiring to that hacienda with our toes in the swimming pool. It's brilliant, if I may say so myself. One set of guys taking

British Columbia's best marijuana to Washington, and another set bringing American hard stuff up here. It's the perfect cover. Cops don't care about a few lousy trails and visitors sneaking around their parks. And by the time they do, we'll be gone. Gone south. Way south, you and me."

Peter could feel his breathing coming rapidly, was suddenly very aware of his stiff limbs. He didn't want to know anything more about these campers. He was out of here. Luckily, he'd never gotten very close anyway. He slipped away as slowly and silently as prey whose life depends on invisibility.

When he knew he was out of hearing range, he looked back one last time, scanned the men's camp quickly to make sure they hadn't seen him. Both men were bent over the campstove, backs to him. Suddenly, injured or not, he was flying away through the forest. As he came within sight of Ron's hammock in the clearing, his legs began to shake and his ribs and shoulders throbbed. It was all he could do to collapse into the mesh sling.

He glanced around camp to make sure he was alone and pressed his knuckles into his forehead. Drug-smuggling backpackers in Cathedral Provincial Park! Wait till he told Ron and Jake! Good thing the men hadn't seen him. Lucky he hadn't walked right into their camp to talk to them, like he'd first intended.

What a scoop! He and Jake and Ron would report it, get the guys caught, stop a big ring, and be proclaimed heroes by the police, the park rangers, television stations, the FBI, CIA, RCMP, and — what was the Canadian spy organization called? — CSIS. He'd be on television!

Excitement coursed through Peter's body as he helped himself to some lemonade, sore limbs forgotten for the moment. He glanced at his watch and looked eagerly up the trail. No sign of Ron and Jake. What a day it had been already! Surviving a major crash, seeing wild mountain goats, being stalked by a cougar, and uncovering a drug operation! The cougar! He'd almost forgotten about the twig snapping and the feeling of being watched. Was it a cougar or some other wild animal or just his imagination? Ron must know whether cougars were a problem up here. Peter would press him for the truth.

Maybe he'd ask Ron about that even before spilling the story of the neighboring campers. If a cougar was stalking the camp, Ron would want to know right away. In fact — he forced his mind to slow down a little — maybe he should hold off telling Ron about the drug guys so he couldn't stop Jake and Peter from returning to spy on them. Maybe Jake would be into sneaking off and seeing them himself, helping Peter gather more information. Jake might have better ideas of what to do. He and Jake could play detective, gather all the intelligence they could on these dudes, then present it to Ron. Jake would enjoy the thrill of it, Peter was sure.

He lifted his stiff legs from the hammock to the ground. Jake and Ron would be back any minute now, he thought. He drew the knife from his back pocket, found some onions to chop, and — mindful of the cougar scare earlier, and figuring that some noise might help — began banging pots and pans around in their makeshift kitchen until he'd managed to plop some spaghetti noodles into a pot of boiling water, and warm up some canned spaghetti sauce.

"Mmmm, smells delicious!" Jake said, bursting into camp on his bike with a grin. "Ron, get a load of this. Peter Montpetit can cook when he really, really wants to. Or at least, he can boil water and open cans."

"Yeah, well, I put some cougar scat in your serving for extra protein," Peter teased Jake back.

"You don't say!" Ron said, pulling up beside Jake and eyeing the bubbling red sauce. "Fresh or vintage scat?"

"Ron," Peter addressed him, hands on his hips and looking him straight in the eyes, "are cougars a problem here?"

Ron's blue eyes studied Peter's face, maybe even caught a tremor in the hand holding the cooking ladle.

"Why?"

"Something has been slinking around camp all afternoon, keeping out of sight. And I swear I could feel it watching me."

Ron said nothing. He touched the knife in his knife belt, reshouldered his pack, and headed into the brush with the words, "Go ahead and serve up, boys. Save mine. I won't be long."

8   Spies

The minute Ron had left, Jake felt Peter tug on his shirt. He turned to see his buddy place a finger over his lips and motion him to a flat boulder on a high point from which they could see Ron's retreat.

"Jake, got to tell you something big," he whispered, eyes scanning the forest around them as if trees could hear. Then, words tumbling over one another in rapid succession, Peter told him a wild tale of stumbling across drug smugglers in the woods. Jake raised his eyebrows, shook his head in wonder. He believed Peter alright, but he couldn't help marveling over how close his crazy friend had come to being seen by these guys. They didn't sound like campers with whom anyone but the police should tangle.

Trying to focus on Peter's words rather than on his black eye, newly scarred chin, and bruised arms and legs, Jake shook his head when Peter started going on about how they should spy on these guys together before reporting them to Ron.

"Are you crazy?" Jake asked. "Why would we do that? If we get in trouble, Ron wouldn't even know where we were."

That launched Peter into a new hyperactive burst of words. Jake had to smile. Peter was nothing if not determined to win his way, and though Jake was trying not to admit it, the notion of seeing these campers for himself was tempting. The boys could always pretend to be hikers just passing by.

"You're trying to wear me down with motor-mouthing so that I'll agree just to make you shut up."

Peter smiled at this. "Hey, whatever works."

His enthusiasm was altogether too contagious for Jake.

"Look, let's think about it, talk later tonight, and decide for sure by the morning," Jake said. "We can't do anything about it tonight anyway so all I'm agreeing to is not saying anything to Ron this evening."

He watched the victory grin spread across Peter's face, then shivered in the gathering dusk. Drug runners in Cathedral Provincial Park, camped not far away, and Ron out looking for a cougar that may have been stalking Peter. What more adventure could they ask for?

An hour later, Ron returned with a scowl and opened his fist to show the boys some dried animal scat.

"Cougar," he declared, sending a shiver up Jake's spine. Jake saw Peter's face pale a little. "You'll probably never see the creature, and it's highly unlikely it'll jump you. It's just trying to live up here, same as we're trying to pass through. It has no argument with us, mostly eats deer. But now you can identify its signs, and here's what you need to know in the unlikely event you see one. Make eye contact; let it know that you know it's there. Never run, crouch, or turn your back. Make yourself tall, wave your arms, and if it comes closer, throw rocks or sticks. Okay? But no cougar has ever leaped anyone in this park, and even in regions where it does happen, most attacks are on children under twelve."

Jake shuddered. His sister Alyson's age. He didn't feel comforted by Ron's speech.

Then, Ron slung away the scat and marched back to camp. "I need a beer," he mumbled. He kicked gear around, ate his supper, and retired to his tent early without so much as a good night to the boys. "Where's a beer when you need one?"

Good thing for us he doesn't have any beer up here, Jake thought. Just as he looked up to see Peter give him the sign to escape camp for a private talk, Ron's voice roared from the tent at a volume that stopped both boys in their tracks.

"Filthy little thief! Should've let the cops have you at the hardware store! You've been sneaking into my tent!"

Jake, stunned, looked accusingly at Peter.

"I … just … wanted to play your harmonica," Peter stuttered. "I … didn't touch … anything else."

Jake moved away from Peter and turned his back as he felt anger and sadness stir. He wasn't sure he believed Peter.

"Don't even think about leaving camp tonight!" came Ron's threatening voice. "You boys are going nowhere."

Jake turned just enough to see Peter's shoulders stoop. Both knew they couldn't dare talk about matters in their tent, even in whispers, only feet away from Ron's tent. Worse, though, Jake no longer felt like talking. Why would Peter go into Ron's tent? Jake sighed. Didn't matter now. Peter was in deep trouble. Ron wouldn't cut him an inch of slack now and that black mood of his looked like it might last awhile.

Half an hour later, as Jake lay in his sleeping bag in the dark with his back to Peter, Peter whispered, "I touched only his harmonica, Jake. Honest. I swear that's all."

Jake didn't speak or turn. What was the point? He

tried to sleep, but his mind went into overdrive as he contemplated Peter's discovery of the campers nearby. What should they do? As he lay awake for hours that night, Jake tingled with both excitement and worry.

The sun had barely cracked the horizon when Jake felt Peter's elbow in his ribs.

"Mmmmm," Jake moaned sleepily.

"Time for an early morning stretch," Peter whispered in his ear.

Jake's eyes struggled to open as he lifted his watch to his face.

"Whaaa? It's 5:30, you idiot. Go back to sleep."

"Not a chance. We're going for a little walk, so quietly that we won't wake the boss. Then we'll return and make breakfast for him, put him in a great mood for the day."

Jake closed his eyes and tried pulling his sleeping bag over his head, but that just prompted Peter to start dripping water from his water bottle on Jake's hair.

"Alright, alright, I'm awake," Jake grumped.

"Shhhhhh."

"Yeah, yeah."

The two rose, dressed, and exited their pup tent soundlessly, then headed away from camp, Peter leading. When they had walked for about fifteen minutes, Jake asked, "How's your body this morning?"

"Sore as heck, but on the mend," Peter replied.

"The skin around your left eye is green instead of black this morning," Jake teased. "Should have iced it yesterday."

"With what?"

"Oh, holding your whole head underwater in the creek for ten minutes or so would have done it."

"Shhhh."

Jake paused as Peter held up his hand and moved behind a tree. Jake followed suit, but not before he'd glimpsed two bodies curled up in sleeping bags well ahead.

"No one's up, surprise, surprise," Jake observed in a hushed voice. "So what are we trying to accomplish here, exactly?"

In reply, Peter clamped his hand over Jake's mouth and pointed. Jake looked, just in time to see a head, shoulders, and hand emerge from one of the sleeping bags. Jake and Peter crouched down low and peered out from behind a bush. Jake scanned the area. A tiny, one-pot backpackers' stove, a small bag of supplies, and two daypacks were strewn about. Two guys sleeping in the open with no more than one or two days' supplies, he calculated. Normal backpackers would have much larger packs.

Another arm emerged, then a tall and powerfully built man shed the sleeping bag and stumbled to the edge of the clearing, his back to the boys. He returned, pulled his jeans on over his boxers, buckled a belt around his muscular waist, and stuffed his feet into a pair of boots. Jake's mouth dropped open as the man reached to the ground and picked up a large steel knife, which he plunged into a sheath on his belt with practiced hands.

Then, with no warning, he applied a swift and vicious kick to the sleeping bag beside his, which prompted a pained cry from within it. Jake couldn't help wincing and crouching lower behind the bush.

"Get up, lazy," the towering figure growled loud enough for the boys to hear. "Get up and make us something to eat."

Peter looked at Jake. Jake looked at Peter. The presence and size of the tough's knife had stunned them both. It was definitely not for cutting onions.

"Let's get out of here," Jake whispered so low that he wasn't sure Peter would make out the words. He was relieved when Peter nodded in agreement. They began to crawl and slither away in an army-style retreat, Jake leading this time. But Jake stopped abruptly as his hand touched something rubbery sticking out from a pile of brush. He lifted his hand, looked, and blinked. A bike tire. Make that a bike rim. Make that two full-suspension mountain bikes, painstakingly hidden beneath branches and grass.

Jake turned his head and watched Peter look, and his eyes widen. These guys weren't backpackers. They were bikers — with bikes exactly the same make and brand as Ron's, Jake's, and Peter's.

Before he could register another thought, Jake heard the big man's voice ring out. "Hank! Go get the bikes. It's getting late!"

Jake didn't need anyone to tell him what to do at that point. The boys were on a knoll behind some thick brush, a sixty-second downhill dash from there to the next line of bushes and trees. In one swift move, Jake dived, rolled, and crawled to the lower stand of foliage, Peter hardly a breath behind him. They were well out of sight by the time a short, slightly stocky man appeared on the knoll, glanced around, and began uncovering the bikes. Good thing the twig and pine needle–strewn ground didn't leave footprints, Jake thought, as his heart thumped and his breath came in rapid bursts.

Hank. Ron's high school friend? Hank, the one who'd been "livin' rough"? If so, that made the other man Laszlo, the one Ron had described as "a nasty piece of work." Unwanted thoughts began to crowd

Jake's brain. He pushed them away to concentrate on getting out of this place undetected.

The moment Hank had disappeared with the bikes, Jake and Peter left the brush and sprinted back to camp. As they drew near, Jake was relieved to note that Ron wasn't up yet. He felt Peter's hand on his arm.

"Jake, we're not saying anything to Ron, right? We have to talk about this, right?"

"Yes," Jake mumbled, head hung low.

9   Conference at the Ravine

Ow could they break away from Ron long enough to talk, and be certain that their boss wouldn't overhear? Jake wondered as Ron, who was in a particularly foul mood, drove them like a maniacal foreman. The breakfast hadn't soothed the awful temper one bit as they prepared for the day.

"Stop slacking. We've got to get real mileage on this trail today," he shouted in a voice that made both boys shrink. "I've been way too easy on you. You're both of you working like wimps," he added, eyes flashing such fire that Jake doubled his efforts.

Jake was busy opening a lemonade mix packet to go with their sandwiches at lunchtime when Ron added, "And I want you two to stick around over your lunch break today."

Jake tensed. Ron had never asked that before. This must be his way of punishing Peter for snooping around, but it was so unfair! And it was going to make it even more difficult for the boys to discuss what they'd seen and heard earlier that morning. They hadn't had a minute out of earshot of Ron yet.

"We're behind schedule by at least a day," Ron continued in an explosive voice. "Trail has to be finished on Monday."

"Has to be finished on Monday *or what?*" Peter challenged. Was Peter on a suicide mission to butt heads with Ron or something? "Your buddies signed up clients without the trail even being built? Why should that be our problem? Jake and I have busted our butts for you for five days straight now — no sleeping in, two little breaks a day for real riding, just half of one afternoon off after we worked double hard to earn it."

"Peter, shut your trap before I shove this dirty towel down it," said Ron, pronouncing the words distinctly as if every ounce of self-control he had was being used to keep himself in check. "You're the whiniest, laziest, most dishonest child I've ever had the rotten luck to supervise. One more peep and I'll put you on kitchen duty morning, noon, and night."

Jake watched Peter's jaw work back and forth, but his buddy wisely held his tongue as Jake handed him the thermos of lemonade to shake up.

Seating himself on a boulder behind them, Jake

picked up a package of stale cookies he was about to add to their lunch pack and passed it to Peter, hoping that might occupy his big mouth for a little while.

Could Ron know they were dying to get away from him to talk, even for a few minutes?

"Done with packing lunch?" Ron interrupted Jake's train of thought.

"Yes, done," Jake replied.

"*Then get doing the breakfast dishes,*" Ron shouted at Peter, making both boys jump in surprise. Why was Ron being so mean? Jake wondered. Could he sense their new wariness of him, their quandary over whether he was innocent or untrustworthy? Jake yearned for Ron's kinder, lighter side to return. And he worried, as he was sure Peter was worrying, about whether the "Hank" in the camp was Ron's friend Hank. If so, did that mean Ron knew the men were around, knew they might be plotting to use the bike trail to smuggle drugs back and forth between the United States and Canada? Jake, for one, definitely didn't believe Ron was in on this with his friends and using Jake and Peter to build a drug-running trail.

"Get!" Peter shouted, tossing dirty dishwater in the direction of a deer that had appeared near their tents. Ron and Jake looked at each other. Jake wondered how much grumpier everyone could get. And he wondered what he could do to put things right.

"Peter, I'll help you dry dishes so we can get to work," he suggested. "We can have some time off after supper, right, Ron?"

Ron looked up, jaw set, and for a minute, Jake was certain he wasn't going to let them.

"Work harder today and I'll say yes," he answered, picking up a rock and pitching it at a tree like an angry baseball player.

"Hey, thanks," Peter said, brightening a little. Eight hours of hard labor later, Jake was almost too spent to make chili for supper that evening, but Ron, who hadn't lightened up all day, made no move to help him with supper. As they ate their chili in silence, Jake felt his body reviving, especially knowing he and Peter could escape camp at last. Ten minutes after they'd finished dishes, they were off, wheeling to freedom, however short-lived that would have to be. When they reached the jump, Peter paused.

"Let's play here on our way back," he suggested rather loudly. Then he lowered his voice. "We need to get further away to talk." Resuming his normal voice, he said, "I feel like doing some distance first. Okay with you?"

"Sure," Jake replied, annoyed that Peter seemed to think Ron would eavesdrop on them, but not in the mood for the jump anyway. He pedaled behind Peter to a point well beyond where their day's work had halted. Peter, somewhat recovered from his crash the day before, spun over the uneven ground with a confidence and speed Jake hadn't witnessed since their North Shore ride.

"Slow down, Peter. You're gutting me," Jake protested.

Peter smiled and reached for his water bottle, then frowned. "Empty," he said, crinkling the bottle before shoving it back into its holder and looking behind them once again. "Let's head down this stone shoulder to the right and check out that gully. Must be some water there."

Jake examined the seam of granite that shot off from their path down a reasonable slope to a faraway fold between trees. Yes, it probably held a creek bed, and, yes, the exposed bedrock formed an inviting path that seemed to promise a relatively safe bike descent. Not to mention some privacy for talking over what had been eating at both of them for twelve hours.

"Lead on, guide," he directed.

Peter flashed a smile, touched his feet to his pedals, and spun away. Following just a few bike lengths behind, Jake concentrated on holding his tires to the granite slope, admiring how it dropped them quickly and smoothly toward the huddle of trees not far below. Well, almost smoothly. He heard Peter shout a warning and saw Peter's bike catch some air over an unexpected set of jagged rocks that resembled stairs on the route.

Jake pulled up on his handlebars to bring the front wheel up in time and gritted his teeth as if that would guarantee traction on the dusty granite landing below the steps. Ouch. Not so great on the private parts, but a good show of fast reactions in the face of challenge, he decided.

Jake opened his mouth to tell Peter to stop and wait but saved his breath when he saw Peter slow down, stare ahead, then ride his bike onto a giant log over a short gully. Had he gone nuts? Log rides were fine on carefully constructed courses, but this was as far off the beaten path as they could get. This was no time for exploratory stuff. Hadn't Peter learned his lesson after all?

Nope. He continued along the bleached white log like a high-wire rider. Jake reached the log, dismounted, and wrung his hands.

"Jake, come on over. Absolutely safe, a great ride," came Peter's voice from the far side of the log. A grassy hill sloped downward, soaking up the rosy hues of the evening's sunshine. Jake eyed the log and had to agree that close up, it looked a lot safer than constructions he'd survived. Wider, no higher, and pine cones so plentiful six feet below that he suspected he'd bounce like a trampoline jumper if he did topple off. Jake backed up and went for it.

"Sweet!" Peter enthused as the two did high-fives and dumped their bikes on the grass at the far side. They sat down, pulled out granola bars, and lay back, feet resting against a smooth rock ledge over a new, second, and much deeper ravine, this one containing a thirsty creek far below.

"We're not going to make it way down there to fill your water bottle," Jake observed.

"I've noticed. But it's a perfect conference spot." Silence reigned as each waited for the other to start.

"It's not necessarily the same Hank," Jake began. His heart felt like it had slipped down his chest to lie lifeless against his gut as he said it.

"Not necessarily," Peter repeated. His pause, and the fact he wouldn't look Jake straight in the eyes, squeezed Jake's chest.

"If they're Ron's friends, if they're his bosses on this trail, why would they be camped nearby and not come to talk to him?"

Jake watched Peter cup his chin in his hands and stare vacantly into the distance.

"Maybe they don't know he's mentioned them to us? And they'd rather we don't see them."

"Or," Jake pulled himself into a cross-legged position, "he doesn't know they're there, doesn't know they want to use the trail for drugs, and they're spying on him and seeing how the trail is coming along."

"Maybe." Jake could tell from Peter's tone that he wasn't buying all of that.

"So we should warn Ron. He'd never get mixed up in illegal stuff."

"But he's lied to us a couple of times already to get us up here, and he's turned real mean the last day. We don't know him, Jake. We don't know how far he's in. I think we should get the heck out of this park, without saying a word to him."

"No way. He hired us to do a job. We'd be leaving him high and dry, and if these guys are hovering around to give him the gears and we bail out, he'll be in bad trouble, and we wouldn't be around to help him."

Peter picked up a handful of pine cones, moved to the far end of the rock saddle on which they were sitting, and began to toss them into the creek bed far below.

"Ron's not our responsibility, Jake. We need to look after ourselves. Open your eyes. Look what he's gotten us into."

"Yeah, well, even if I agreed we should cut out on him after all he's done for us, how do you know those guys won't chase us, cut us off from making it back to Keremeos?" Jake could tell from the clouded look that crossed Peter's face that his friend hadn't thought of that.

"Ever heard of innocent till proven guilty, Peter? You're not giving Ron the benefit of the doubt. And that's pretty ironic, given what he did for you at the hardware store." Jake leaped up and started pacing, but kept one eye on Peter's face. He'd gotten Peter this time, he could tell. Bull's-eye.

"I ..." Peter started, but stopped.

"You, me, Ron, we're a team. If there are drug runners camped near us, Ron needs to know. If they're his friends, he needs to know what they're up to so all three of us can get out of here safely and report them. If they're nearby because they want to keep an eye on Ron, he needs to know that, too, Peter. He gave you a chance. Go with your gut feeling. You don't know Ron well, but you know he'd never, ever put us in danger, right? Go with your gut on that, Peter."

Peter's face represented a fierce internal battle. Jake watched him pick up a smooth rock and squeeze it. Jake let him be, didn't push.

Finally, Peter turned to Jake. "My gut says you're right that he wouldn't knowingly put us in danger. But the rest doesn't add up. My gut also says you're seeing him through rose-colored glasses, Jake. You want to believe he's more honest than he may be. But you're right about the second-chance thing. If it weren't for Ron, I'd have a police record right now. So I owe him the same: doing what it takes to make sure he doesn't get one *if* he's innocent. So okay, we'll level with him when we get back. And I'll be watching his face closely." Peter's face was dead serious when he said that.

Jake felt his heart go light, felt it float back up his chest. He smiled. It was the right thing to do — he hoped.

Peter finished the granola bar he'd placed beside him as they'd begun to talk, flipped onto his stomach, and crawled to the edge of the rock lip to hang his head over the deep streambed.

"Yikes!" he said, retreating a little.

Jake inched forward to join him, remembering Peter was a little afraid of heights. He had to give him credit for his bravery, given what lay in front of them: a six-foot-deep gully under the log they'd just crossed and a twenty-foot-deep ravine immediately in front of them. Jake spit down into the ravine. So, he thought, the little grassy ramp on which they were resting was an island, sort of. He was surprised to feel blood rushing to his head from the steepness of the ramp. He gripped the rock edging like someone riding in the shovel of a bulldozer aimed to tip its load into the trickle of water two stories below and glanced at Peter, whose knuckles were looking a little white.

"Whoa, wouldn't want to ride off this shelf," Jake asserted. Not that they'd been in any danger of doing so when they'd come off the log and crawled down the ramp to here.

Peter, instead of answering, gritted his teeth and lifted his head to examine the dirt bank twenty feet across the ravine.

"If this was the Shore, someone would smooth that dirt transition on the other side, and some maniac would jump the creek," he observed.

"And break lots of bones or die if he missed it," Jake inserted, "though there are so many wacko riders on the Shore it wouldn't make a dent in the downhill-biking population."

"In fact, it's almost a natural transition the way it is," Peter continued.

"Don't say it." Jake grabbed Peter by his T-shirt and pulled him away from the lip. "I promised Ron I'd keep you under control."

Peter laughed and pulled Jake's hand off his T-shirt. "Did I say we were going to do it? Relax, old buddy. I was just observing, like any intelligent down-hiller, that it's doable, right? A twenty-foot gap, nice smooth ramp feeding onto a rock saddle this side, and on the other side, a nice soft dirt landing heading downhill, starting five feet lower. What more could a radical rider ask for?"

Jake resumed his grip on Peter's shirt and pulled him backwards up the stone saddle to the grass.

"Okay, okay, Mom, I'm coming," said Peter. "I admit, it's no place to fill a water bottle. Anyway, Uncle Ron's going to start worrying about us, and if we don't get back before dark, he'll ground us or something. Then we won't have time to spill the beans to him — quietly," he added with force, "in case our camp has eavesdroppers. The dirt jump will have to wait till tomorrow," he added with disappointment.

The two wheeled their bikes up the grassy slope and negotiated the log back to the granite seam, this time with greater confidence. As they attempted to ride the seam back up to the deer trail, they started sliding backwards.

"Hate dismounting and walking my bike," Peter complained.

They reached camp just before dark. Only problem was, camp was empty. There was no sign of Ron or, they determined after a quick search, his bike or backpack. His tent, tools, the food supplies, and stove remained.

"So he's gone out for a little ride," Jake said uneasily.

Peter fetched his headlamp and began circling the camp, walking in ever wider circles, casting his light on the ground as he worked his way ever farther into the darkening woods. Jake kept calling, "Ron," but there was no answer.

After half an hour's search, during which they jumped every time they heard the underbrush crackle, they returned to camp.

"Peter, here's his harmonica, with a note under it," Jake declared. How had they missed that?

Peter joined Jake beside the boulder the three had been using as a picnic table and cast his light on the paper as Jake held it up.

Boys: I've ridden back to Keremeos to get some supplies. I'll be back in a day or two. Please carry on with the trail. I've left some pink tape to mark the next section. Ron

Jake was so relieved that Ron hadn't been pounced on by a cougar that he sat down on a rock and ran a hand across his forehead. "A day or two," he repeated, frowning. "Guess we'd better not slack off or he'll have our heads when he returns. New supplies will mean some fresh food for once," he added, licking his lips. "We *were* pretty low."

"I envy him the ride down to town, but not the ride back up, especially with a heavy pack," Peter added. "But how come he didn't mention this at suppertime?"

Jake didn't like the unsettled tone of Peter's voice, or the sense that Peter might be relieved that he was off the hook for telling Ron about the men.

"'Cause he was in a rotten mood. Or he decided it on the spur of the moment, maybe discovered we were low on something essential and made up his mind to do the dash before dark." Jake shrugged his shoulders, chin thrust out and arms crossed. "Like you'd be someone who doesn't understand spur of the moment decisions. Let's crash. I'm tired."

"Not before I've had a go on the harmonica," Peter said.

"Suit yourself," Jake replied and crawled into the tent. For ten minutes, he put up with Peter's less than musical attempts to serenade them. It shouldn't be a big deal, camping one night without Ron. But Jake missed the man's presence, if not his more tuneful harmonica playing.

Eventually, much to Jake's relief, Peter gave up and crawled inside the tent. After a ridiculous amount of shuffling around, he finally got himself inside his bag and clicked off his headlamp. Within ten minutes, a sleepy Jake registered two sounds: Peter's heavy breathing and the crackling of twigs nearby.

"Deer," Jake told himself. But it took him hours to fall asleep.

10   Questions

"Let's move camp," Peter declared the following morning, as he and Jake finished a late breakfast following a short sleep-in.

"No way. Wait till Ron gets back," Jake replied.

Peter drummed his fingers on the boulder beside him, glanced around their clearing, eyed their tent. How could he tell Jake what was on his mind? How could he sway Jake to consider what he was thinking? How could he express the growing sense that they might be in danger, might need to be prepared for a quick getaway? He couldn't banish the picture of the big brute's knife. Yes, he wanted to give Ron the benefit of the doubt, but he also wanted to cover other bases in this game. That's what Jake wasn't doing. And what of this new twist, Ron's disappearance? Would he really have taken off to buy food when he was so worried about finishing the trail? He clearly trusted

Jake to get on with the trail, but Peter didn't feel he had Ron's full trust any more, so it seemed all the stranger that Ron would suddenly leave the boys alone, even just for a day. Not that *Jake* doubted the contents of Ron's note for a second, of course.

Jake, Mr. Honest and Trusting. Jake, Mr. Workaholic. Jake, who seemed to want Ron to be his dad. No, he figured, Jake wouldn't hear him out. He'd have to spend more time building his case, plotting strategy. Jake's loyalty to Ron was a problem. Best to take this slowly. And he had to be very, very careful what he said and when. But he would bring Jake around to his plan, somehow.

"You're right," Peter said. "We'll wait till Ron is back this afternoon. I'm guessing he'll agree it's time to move closer to our worksite, so I'm going to organize our gear for that now."

Jake shrugged. "Suit yourself. I'll make sandwiches. Can't wait for fresh bread tonight. This stuff is pretty stale."

As Jake turned his back, Peter entered their tent, dumped out the contents of both his and Jake's backpacks, and stuffed their two sleeping bags into his backpack, happy that both were the kind that packed down very small. He then placed all nonessentials, including their extra clothing and books, into a plastic bag, which he rested by a nearby tree. Next, he collapsed the pup tent and rolled it into as compact a bundle as he could. With a little effort, he managed to stuff that and their headlamps into his backpack as well, which he propped up in full sight on top of a stump at the edge of the clearing.

Carrying Jake's empty backpack over to his buddy's workspace, Peter said, "Hey, thanks for making the sandwiches. Let's put them in your pack today." As Jake dropped the sandwiches in, Peter added, "Looks like we're ready for the trail. Let's show Ron how hard we can work even without his supervision."

Jake smiled and walked over to climb onto his bike.

Peter let Jake lead as they headed out of camp so he wouldn't notice that Peter had left his backpack behind and wouldn't catch him turning his head to glance behind them regularly.

It was a crisp, clear, and cool day. Surrounding peaks glittered in the morning light. What an excellent day for a ride, Peter thought, catching air wherever a bump or bank allowed him, and looking forward to pulling a few tricks on the dirt jump. The fun part about the morning commute was knowing every inch of the trail, never mind appreciating the hard work it had taken to clear it. When they reached the five-foot-high piles of dirt, Peter patted them proudly.

"Think Ron will leave these up for the tours' more adventurous clients?" Jake asked.

So, Peter thought, stubborn Jake has gone back to believing Ron is building a trail for legitimate bike tours. He sighed.

"If he does, he should pay us overtime, since it took us three hours of our off-time. Are you okay with ten minutes of play before we go to the worksite?"

"Sure," Jake said.

Peter began by performing a few nose manuals, then circled around and made sure Jake was looking before sprinting up and off the first lip and executing the suicide no-hander he'd been perfecting. Up he flew, clapped his hands behind his back, whipped them back to his handlebars before it was too late.

"Whoa! Take it easy before you crash again," Jake called out, clearly impressed.

"Jake, want to see my Superman?"

"You can't do a Superman, and this isn't the place even if you could. We've got no body armor or full-face helmets, in case you've forgotten." With that, Jake performed a suicide one-hander, looking to Peter as if expecting applause.

"Not bad, old buddy," Peter said, "but pull over; you're in the slow lane!" Peter noticed apprehension and disapproval written all over his friend's face. This only made Peter accelerate some more. He shot up the lip like a loosed torpedo, buying tons of air. Hands choking his handlebars, he lifted his entire body off the bike in one swift move until it was nearly flat above it like a banner whipping in the wind. Getting his feet back on the pedals before he hit the off-ramp was nothing like as easy as he'd hoped, and the landing was "sketch." But he held it together, just, and managed to keep from falling before he stopped.

"Yes!" he shouted, arms raised in victory, as Jake pulled up, shaking his head.

"You're my hero," Jake joked, but the slap he applied to Peter's back felt entirely genuine.

"Now all I need to get is my ..."

"... Superman seat grab. Yeah, right. Not in a million years, Peter. What are you on, anyway? And where's your backpack?"

"Oops. Forgot it. But we have the sandwiches in yours, so we're okay. And it's time to go to work, for sure. Let's show Ron what his employees are made of."

Jake's smile indicated he'd fallen for that, and they peeled away from the jump.

Peter felt so jubilant about having pulled off a Superman that he could hardly keep his tires on the road. They carried on, bantering about their favorite downhill mountain bike athletes, Jake leading. They passed the granite seam that left the trail and shot down to the ravine. It was great to shake out the stiffness of a cold night's camping. Even a week into their job, Peter continued to be amazed by how hot it could

be during the day, and how cold at night at this elevation. As he and Jake muscled their way up a steep rise,
Peter eased into the first phase of his plan.

"Hey, Jake, let's do a quick side trip up at the top
and get our bearings."

Jake halted on the ridge and waited for Peter to pull
up. They dropped their bikes and walked to a rise that
showcased an entire world of pristine mountains.

"What a view, hey?" Peter took in the panorama of
forested slopes, which rose and fell for dozens of miles
ahead.

"Not a road, house, or farm in sight," Jake mur-
mured. "Even the lakes look like puddles from here.
It's like looking down from an airplane."

"Yup," Peter said. He pointed southwest at a snow-
capped mountain head and shoulders above the rest.

"There's Mt. Baker, nearly seventy-five miles away.
And Mt. Logan, closer in to us."

He turned straight south and shaded his eyes. "The
big one immediately in front of us is Mt. Remmel, but
look a little west of that, about as far as you can see,
and that's got to be Big Craggy Peak. It sits where the
Pasayten Wilderness touches the Okanogan National
Forest, only twenty miles north of Winthrop, where
my grandparents live. Pretty much everything in
front of us is in Washington State, I'd guess."

"Mmmm, I'd been thinking we must be close to

the border. What happens if a hiker goes across the border, anyway? How would anyone know?" Jake wondered aloud. "Think they have trip wires or hidden cameras around?"

Peter broke into laughter. "Jake, old buddy, it's the largest unsecured border in the world. They're not going to spend tax dollars monitoring this terrain. But anyone who goes across the border where there isn't a guard to check in with is required to call in as soon as they get to a phone. It's an honor system, spot-checked by the occasional plane or spy, I suppose."

"Oh yeah? And how would you know that?" Jake asked, stern face turning to Peter.

"My dad told me. Pilots have to know stuff like that."

"Oh."

"Race you to the worksite," Peter challenged. The two sprinted back to their bikes. Before Jake could lift his feet to his pedals, Peter sprinted down the slope ahead, letting a cloud of dust slow his friend. This was sweet riding, especially with some of his home state's finest scenery spread before him. For a minute or two, Peter let the past two days' tensions and questions evaporate as he drank in the awesome terrain: peaks, valleys, creeks, crags, and turquoise lakes winking at him in the rising heat. It was a glorious day to tear down a fresh-built trail, knowing exactly where he could rip up a bank and jump down again, leap over a small ditch, and skid around corners. Unfortunately, the day's worksite came all too soon. Reluctantly, Peter dropped his bike and dragged his feet over to the pile of tools. That's when he noticed the first strip of pink plastic tape flapping in the breeze from a tree branch.

"Just like Ron said, markers to tell us where we go from here," Jake noted with satisfaction.

Peter frowned. How had Ron managed to ride down here, do all this tape-hanging, then head to Keremeos, all before dark last night? And all without a mention of his plan at suppertime?

"I'll do the ax work first shift," Peter offered. He needed something to hit while putting the final touches on his plan. He'd show Jake how hard he could work. But only until noon.

By the time the sun was frying them from straight overhead, both boys were ravenous. Peter was relieved when Jake laid aside his tools and moved to some shade. The two drank heavily from their water bottles and stuffed their sandwiches down their gullets like they hadn't eaten for a week.

Peter allowed a quiet stretch to follow. Finally, he spoke.

"Jake," he began his carefully rehearsed speech, "what are the chances a provincial park would really, truly allow commercial downhill mountain biking?"

Jake's water bottle stopped mid-air. "Some allow cross-country skiing, some allow horse packing. Why not?"

"Jake, I want to ask you a few questions. Will you promise to let me ask them before you get your back up?"

Peter watched Jake turn to him, eyes narrowed. When Peter refused to proceed, he finally muttered, "Shoot, then."

"First question: Why won't Ron tell his friends we want to be guides?"

"We're not old enough." Jake's voice was impatient.

"Yet we've both worked for Sam's Adventure Tours. Don't you think it implies he knows what his so-called friends are really up to?"

When Jake didn't reply, Peter went on. "Next question: Why are the clients' bikes outfitted with army camouflage satchels?"

Jake jumped up and paced, kicked a stone away. "Looks cool, I guess. Or maybe there was a sale on camouflage packs! Come on, Peter, I thought you'd promised to give Ron the benefit of the doubt."

"Ron, maybe, but not his friends. If his friends are drug smugglers, camouflage packs for their riders would be perfect. We're trying to figure out, aren't we, how much Ron knows and how long he's known it?"

Peter watched Jake bury his head in his hands.

"I have three more questions to go, Jake. Just three. You promised to hear me out."

Jake crossed his arms, backed away two steps, and threw Peter a look that seemed to dare him to lob more questions.

"Jake, why won't Ron ever let us see his map, or give us a straight answer about where we're heading? Why did he forbid us from bringing cameras, binoculars, compasses, cellphones, and other sundries? And why would two teams build a trail from two ends and meet up in the middle?"

"It worked for the Chunnel," Jake said loudly, spitting at the dirt.

"Yes, because it was being tackled by teams from two different countries, meeting on a border between. Jake, do you know what camouflage bags full of drugs would be worth? Thousands and thousands of dollars on the street. Fix two satchels on each bike, maybe add more in the rider's backpack, and each and every bike courier on this trail would probably score six figures *per trip*. How many bikes did Ron have in that garage, Jake? And you wonder why Ron is paying us well to help finish off the trail? It's him, not his friends, who decided how much to pay us. I'm not saying for sure he knows all that's going down, but my gut tells me he's not dumb, and if he's not back when we get to camp, let's use the chance to get away while we can."

Jake stared at Peter, face white, eyes bulging, mouth terse. Peter waited, shaking a little inside, not sure what kind of fuse he had just lit, or what it would do next. Jake had looked so relieved back when Peter had agreed to talk to Ron about the guys in the woods, but ever since then, Peter had had a hard time sticking with the notion that it was a good idea. Too many things didn't connect, especially since Ron had disappeared. As Peter was trying to decide how to persuade Jake to his view that they needed to escape, Jake walked toward his bike and picked it up. Peter feared he was going to ride off, or head back to camp without him. He'd counted on being able to reason with Jake enough that he wouldn't do that. Now he wasn't sure. He watched Jake, back turned to him, gripping the handlebars of his trembling bike.

After several long moments, he dropped the bike and stalked back to face Peter, who remained seated, palms sweaty.

"It takes a dishonest person to imagine dishonesty in someone else, Peter. I should have known when you gave me that muffin that things were too changed for us to be friends anymore. You're not giving Ron a second chance. Why should I give you one? You've turned into more of a jerk than I ever imagined you could. Guess those loser friends of yours in Seattle have pulled you down pretty low. You've been jealous of Ron this entire trip, just because he treats me better than you. But you don't deserve to be treated decently. I know Ron better than you do. He would never, ever be part of a drug-running operation, let alone haul us into it. I'm not sure I want to work with you anymore this trip, not sure I even want to see you again. Why don't you just ride back to Keremeos and I'll tell Ron you're a deserter? He won't be one bit surprised."

Peter sighed. He'd expected this, but he wasn't giving up.

"Jake, you're right that Ron would never knowingly put us in danger. That's why he's told us nothing, refused to share the map with us, and concocted a brilliant story we pretty much bought. But there's only one way he could have known I snuck into his tent that day. The cougar I thought was stalking me wasn't a cougar. I bet it was Ron's bosses. I bet when Ron went looking for the cougar, he ran into them and they told him I'd been in his tent. Maybe they thought he had something in there that would clue us in to them or their game. Anyway, maybe they gave him a seriously hard time for hiring us. I bet Ron never told Hank and Laszlo that he fired the other two workers and hired us for the last ten days' work. But they found out and came to pay Ron a sneak visit.

And found me rummaging through Ron's tent."

"But he brought back cougar scat."

"*Dry* cougar scat," Peter said. "Could've been months old, a cover for where he'd really been. Has he or has he not been a different person since? Has he or has he not been pushing us to finish this trail like his life and ours depended on it, ever since 'my cougar' — Laszlo — decided I might have caught onto the real story? You're right, Jake. He doesn't want us hurt."

Jake spat at the ground again. "I don't buy it, Peter, but what *were* you doing in his tent? What *did* you steal or find out? Why should I trust you on *anything*, after seeing you steal a muffin in North Vancouver and hearing about the pocket knife you tried to steal in Keremeos? And now you admit going into Ron's private stuff. Not to mention you know all about border patrols and what drugs are worth." The sarcasm practically dripped off his tongue.

Peter sighed. "I found nothing, Jake. I don't blame you for not believing me, but I didn't take anything but the harmonica for an hour. So I've shoplifted, but that doesn't compare to what Hank, Laszlo, and maybe Ron are up to. I won't help a drug operation, even if I'm not dead sure that's what's going down here. I don't know whether Ron has gone back to Keremeos for supplies, whether he abandoned us, or whether his 'bosses' have removed him to keep a closer eye on us.

I don't know if he wrote that note and hung the pink tape, or if someone else did both for him. I just think you need to know that *I* think we could be in danger."

Jake spun around and stomped back to his bike, shouldered his backpack, and swung a leg over his crossbar. "Get out of this park, Peter. Leave us alone. I'm headed back to camp to wait for Ron."

And before Peter could say a word, before he could breathe through a sudden, very tight constriction in his throat, Jake took off in the direction they'd come, leaving Peter very alone.

11   Chase

Jake pedaled fast, sweat pouring down his brow in the mid-afternoon heat. He could feel his breath coming in bursts. He didn't know why he felt compelled to get back to camp quickly. He didn't know, wasn't sure he cared, if Peter would follow him immediately. Chances were good that Ron wouldn't even be back yet, and then what would he do? And even if Ron was there, Jake was supposed to be building a trail, not rushing into camp alone, a bundle of raw nerves and anger. But Jake didn't want to think. He just wanted to ride hard, and toward camp was the only direction he could go.

He pumped his legs as fast as they would go, back up to the crest where they'd paused a few hours ago to look across the border. Border. No, he wouldn't think about Ron being part of it, refused to buy it. Peter was a jerk, jerk, jerk. And he was jealous of Ron.

As he reached the top, he stopped only long enough to aim water down his parched throat and mop his brow. He avoided looking at the scenery, just cursed the broiling power of the sun. Downhill time now. Enough uphill. He plunged down one of the slopes they'd struggled up this morning, back when they were friends. How could Peter change like that, with no warning? How could he not trust Ron? Okay, so maybe he'd said Ron *could* be clean, but it seemed like he'd mostly written off Ron's innocence, Jake told himself stubbornly. As he banked along a turn, he heard a faint sound back up on the crest. Brakes squeaking. So Peter was following him. Or at least, using the trail they'd built to head back to Keremeos, where he belonged.

Jake's tires took the turns, but his soul was flat and motionless. He tried to block all thoughts from his mind. Just follow the trail. Ron will understand, will take care of things. Jake flashed back to the way Ron had treated Peter when he was injured, the time he'd helped Jake with the butterfly, the day he'd helped them build the jump, the evening he'd encouraged Jake on bike tricks. Ron was a good rider. A good man.

Jake barreled through a dust patch, raised a cloud he hoped would choke Peter. They were nearing camp now. Jake's eyes scanned the clearing anxiously, and his heart leaped. Ron was at the campstove, fixing himself a cup of coffee, back turned to the boys. Jake rode right into the center of the clearing, stopped, and turned to see Peter pause beside a stump at the edge of camp. He was lifting the backpack he'd forgotten that morning onto his back.

"Ron's back," Jake called out jubilantly, directing what he hoped was a withering gaze toward Peter. "So much for your theory that he's in on the drug running." He purposely said this loud enough for Ron to hear, and took in the way Peter's face blanched before he turned back around to face Ron.

Now it was Jake's turn to go white. He registered several things. Ron's black eye and the dried blood beneath his nose. The fact that the knife he always wore on his belt was gone. And the movement of a giant of a man, dressed in full body armor and carrying a full-face helmet, coming out from behind a tree near Ron. Jake's throat went dry. It was the bully they'd seen in the camp in the woods. He turned involuntarily toward Peter, only to see Hank, also dressed in bike armor, moving toward Peter.

"Jake, run for it!" Peter shouted as he spun his bike around and accelerated away from the man chasing him by foot. Peter had only one choice of direction to escape Hank, and it wasn't toward Keremeos. Jake turned back toward Ron, knees suddenly so weak he thought he'd drop right there. Ron's face looked pinched. Laszlo, if that's who he was, was one lunge away from Jake now, and for the first time, Jake spotted the knife in his hand.

"Don't move and you won't get hurt," Laszlo growled. Jake had no intention of moving; he could see it was useless. But when Ron suddenly stepped forward to trip the huge man, and the two began wrestling on the ground, Jake's shaking feet seemed to move to his bike pedals of their own accord. He turned his bike around and headed toward the cloud of dirt that marked Peter's route, body shaking so hard he wasn't sure he could keep the bike upright. Hank had gone back into the woods and emerged with his bike and helmet. Jake just managed to beat him onto the trail.

Now it was a threesome cycling at World Cup speed, Jake in the middle. "Keep on Peter's tail," Jake told himself, teeth clenched, feet working like pistons. "Hank is just behind us, but he looks out of shape. Peter and I can outride him."

Where panic had seized up his every muscle only seconds before, Jake now felt totally focused. Nothing mattered but outriding Hank — and Laszlo, if the big bully managed to get free of Ron and join the chase. But how long could they keep this up? What would happen when they ran out of trail? Too bad Peter hadn't been able to head in the other direction, toward Keremeos.

The creek gap. The words came as if Peter had sent them telepathically. Jake watched Peter's bike hurtle down a gradient ahead past their jump. Jake's stomach tightened to a concentrated knot. It was their only chance. It was also insane. As his bike accelerated down the hill, Jake willed himself to breathe. They were approaching the granite slope. He saw Peter's hand lift off his handlebar and jab right for a split second. Jake wrapped his brain around an image of the route, squeezed his handlebars like he was juicing them. He set his jaw, formed an image of Peter and him flying twenty feet through the air and landing on that neat dirt transition the far side of the creek bed. They could do it. He had to believe it. The men wouldn't dare follow. They didn't know it was there, hadn't studied it. It would take them ages to scramble down and up the ravine, and by then, the boys would be well hidden.

It was that or a knife in the back. Knife or gap? Knife or gap? When Peter's bike jumped off the trail and headed down the granite slab, Jake was right behind him. When Peter's bike leaped the stairlike set of rocks, Jake lifted his handlebars seconds later. As Peter's bike started onto the log ride, Jake registered a scream behind him, heard their pursuer's bike crash, heard the cry of a man in pain. Hank hadn't seen the steps in time. One man down, at least for a moment. With any luck, he'd punctured a tire or bent a rim. Jake was sure he'd broken bones, too. But there was no time to glance back. Peter peeled off the log and started down the grassy ramp the very second Jake jumped on the log. The vibrations, imagined or real, entered Jake's body like an electrical current. His knees felt a little weak, but he knew it wasn't the log ride. This log was generously wide, not like the tall, thin boards on Flying Circus. It was knowing what came after the log, knowing he was going to have to accelerate like a madman on that grassy slope where they'd stopped and talked yesterday evening. That's what was unnerving him. *Accelerate, pull head down, lift front wheel, and fly. Picture it. Know you can do it. Picture it, Jake.*

He saw Peter take flight from the corner of his eye but couldn't watch. As he pumped hard down the soft slope, coiling his body for the leap, his eyes had to focus on the stone saddle, his launch pad. And as his arms pulled up and he bought the largest chunk of air he'd ever considered, his eyes sought the long dirt transition. From high in the afternoon air, that landing looked dark, soft, and long, the only kind Jake had a chance of surviving. As gravity pulled him toward it, he bent his elbows out, tensed every muscle, tucked his tongue far back in his mouth, and gritted his teeth as if knowing he would otherwise chop it off.

Whap. Both tires hit together, the rear one only a hair from the edge of the gap. He felt body and bike shudder, begin to skid sideways. He tightened his grip and leaned, desperately trying to hold it all together. Bike, boy, and dirt slid. Jake's face ground in the dirt the last few seconds, till he and his bike lay still in a heap by a stump. Could've been worse, he thought. Could've "cased" my tire on that landing, done a full bike somersault down the landing. Or jumped short and broken every bone in my body. He spit some dirt out of his mouth and raised his head. That's when he witnessed a nightmare he'd replay over and over the next few days: a rider high in the sky, aiming for the landing — aiming, but short. His front wheel hit the wall just below the landing spot and all but crumpled; his dark eyes, even mostly hidden by a full-face helmet, registered full terror. Then he was gone, out of sight, like a bird that had hit a car windshield.

Jake, still lying beneath his bike, waited for the awful sounds of the man's landing, but the ravine and creek drowned them out. His instincts told him to crawl up the transition and look down, but two hands suddenly lifted his bike from him and grabbed him by the scruff of the neck, then dragged both him and his bike up. Peter! Of course, they couldn't take chances.

Hank, if uninjured, might still crawl up to their side of the creek. If Laszlo was still alive, Hank would deal with him. And how did they know if there might be more guys after them? Numbly, Jake hopped back on his bike and followed Peter for another ten minutes, till Peter stopped and motioned to a heavy stand of trees and brush. Jake followed him into the dense foliage, first erasing their trail with deft movements of his boots, then helping Peter hide their bikes and diving down into the brush beside his buddy. Jake wanted to hug Peter, wanted to say thank you, or sorry, or "we made it," but he knew they mustn't say a word, mustn't move as much as a muscle for as long as they could stand it.

And that, as it turned out, was pretty much until dark, when the air turned very cold and Peter wordlessly pulled some pepperoni sticks out of his backpack.

For the umpteenth time since they'd hidden in these trees, Jake's thoughts turned to Ron. What had the bruiser done to Ron? Where was Ron now? But even if he'd dared speak, this was not anguish he could have shared with Peter.

Jake accepted a meat stick and watched as Peter reached into his backpack and unfurled two sleeping bags and a tent. Where had those come from? Jake wondered, grateful to his shivering core.

12   Partner

Peter nudged Jake long before the dark sky showed streaks of morning light. Not that he was an early morning sort, but extraordinary days called for extraordinary starts, and he for one was anxious to blow this joint. Besides, he'd been awake half the night plotting their next move.

"It's too early," Jake mumbled.

"Exactly," Peter replied. "Too early to run into Hank, if he's still game to chase us."

"His bike is toast and he broke a bone or two," Jake mumbled.

"You're dead sure? You saw it?"

"No, just heard it. On the stairs. What about, uh, his buddy?"

"I know I probably shouldn't have taken the risk, but I crawled up there last night and shone my head-lamp on the creek. He was gone. Probably means

Laszlo is alive but in pretty bad shape. It's not likely Hank would leave him to follow us, but we aren't taking any chances." Both boys went silent for a minute. "No one should jump gaps they haven't scouted first," Peter said, voice thick.

"Thanks for the advice," Jake said, forcing his eyes closed again. Peter noticed Jake's white face, saw that Jake didn't know what else to say. He felt pretty horrified by Laszlo's fall himself. Another bout of silence held for a long period.

Finally, Peter crawled out of his sleeping bag and began stuffing it in its holder. "Too risky to head back to Keremeos."

"I know."

"So we're going to do some creek-riding till something else opens up."

"You mean zigzag from one bank to another? Like riding a wet half-pipe and twisting around all the boulders? I guess we can pull that off. There's so little water in it. And it leaves less of a trail for followers, too."

"Exactly. All the way to my grandpa's house if we have to."

"Hey, that's right. On this side of the border, the park is called the Pasayten Wilderness. And it goes south till it's called the Okanogan Forest. And that stops just north of Winthrop."

"And it's got hiking trails. We'll find a way to get

through; maybe we'll eventually run into a hiking party. What we could really use now are those trip wires and cameras on the border you mentioned yesterday. Then a posse of helicopters would be dispatched to pick us up pronto."

"Mmmm. Too bad neither country wastes taxpayers' money on stuff like that."

They packed the sleeping bags and tent into their backpacks, checked their bikes — which were in miraculously good condition considering yesterday's punishment — and felt their way down to the creek's bottom in the near dark, starting well downstream of the gap.

Glancing up nervously once they'd reached the river's bottom, they rode without headlamps, slowly at first. For once, Peter was thankful for the summer's drought, which meant plenty of exposed riverbed and water low enough they could hydroplane through as they crossed from one bank to the other. So they wove down the creek bed from dawn till afternoon, balancing, leaning, curving, drawing figure-eights for many miles. Only occasionally did they have to drag their bikes up the bank and detour around some unnavigable stretches.

"Portage," Peter would joke, a term familiar to them from whitewater kayaking. On one portage, Peter spotted piles of loose rocks on each side of the creek. Curious, he walked over and kicked a little pyramid, but only a few rocks scattered.

"Strong little pile of rocks," he commented. "Doesn't look natural."

"A cairn," Jake said. "A hiker or park ranger has built it to mark this spot."

The two explored until they discovered a line of cairns, each barely within sight of the next.

"I've got it!" Jake enthused. "We're looking at the 49th."

"The 49th?" Peter asked.

"The 49th Parallel, the U.S./Canadian border. Right now, you're in Washington, and I'm in British Columbia."

Peter's brain tugged on this piece of information for a few moments; then it came to him. "4907111. Maybe it wasn't a phone number. Maybe it was a code," he mumbled aloud.

"What wasn't a phone number?" Jake shot Peter a look.

"The scrap of paper I found in Ron's tent. It said '4907111. J.G. (José).' I figured it was a girl's phone number. But how's this for a translation? 49th Parallel. July 11th at one o'clock?"

"That's Monday. But I thought you didn't touch anything except the harmonica."

"It fell out of the tent pocket while I was trying to

find the harmonica. I replaced it right away. Monday is the day we were supposed to finish the trail. Jake, maybe 'José' is the head of the 'Chunnel's' other team, the American trail-making group. Maybe one o'clock is the official meeting time."

"Yeah, well, what good does that do us? It's Friday. We're three days early, we have no idea where their trail is, and I'm not sure we'd want to run into them anyway. And that's assuming it isn't a woman's phone number."

"Guess you're right." Peter hung his head and stared at the cairn. "Except that it *is* a trail, and they don't know who we are, and we need to get to Winthrop."

"What we need is a topographic map, but like you pointed out yesterday, only Ron had one of those."

Peter extended his arm and smiled. "Well, allow me to invite you into the United States, on condition you'll phone in and report your border crossing on your next encounter with civilization."

"Agreed, sir. I guess you're okay, being an American citizen."

"Actually," Peter countered, "I have to phone in, too. And I'm looking forward to doing just that."

With this, they spun back to face north, saluted Canada, then turned their backs on the stunning Cathedral Provincial Park, saluted America, and cycled into the late afternoon of Washington State's lush Pasayten Wilderness, all along the same bony creek. They rode till the day's heat began to let up, stopping now and again for water, rest, shade, and pepperoni sticks.

"I could get tired of these," Jake suggested at one point.

"Hunger is more tiring," Peter responded.

By evening, their trusty stream disgorged into a cold, clear lake that backed up against a tall cliff. They stopped well short of the lake. Peter eyed it nervously from the cover of some bushes. "It'd be so nice to camp and take a dip there, but way too risky."

"Definitely too exposed," Jake agreed, slumping down beside him and taking a long drink of water from his water bottle. "What next? I don't see any natural routes."

Peter was silent a moment, thinking. He swatted at a mosquito, removed his helmet from his sweat-drenched head, and eyed the setting sun.

"Very muggy tonight. Feels like it could rain. Those are pretty much the first gray clouds we've seen all trip. Let's camp right here. We'll maybe take a dip in the lake under cover of darkness."

"Sounds like a plan," Jake said. "Let's see, for supper we have ... wouldn't be pepperoni sticks, would it?"

"You're psychic," Peter responded.

They set up their tent and drew lines in the dirt until they decided they had a chessboard, then gathered twigs and pebbles to assemble a full cast of players. The game lasted until dark, when Jake broke the humid forest's silence with the word, "Checkmate."

"I surrender and respectfully suggest you go jump in a lake," Peter joked. He'd been glancing down there longingly for the past hour. It was super-sticky tonight, like just before a rain shower.

"Excellent idea," Jake said. "It's something, isn't it, being by a lake without a boat, cabin, or trail in sight? Totally wilderness. Totally alone."

"Let's hope." They left their bikes and gear and crept down to the water under cover of darkness. Peter was happy about the moon being a tiny crescent mostly obscured by dark clouds. They stripped and waded in. "Ice cold," Peter whispered as he wriggled his toes in the mucky sediment and let his feet feel their way over sticks embedded there.

"Of course. Fed from snow patches just above us," Jake whispered back. "Hit the water quietly," he instructed as he sliced soundlessly into the water. "Yiii," he whispered as he surfaced. "C-c-cold."

Peter took a deep breath and dived slow-motion to avoid splashing, then slithered back to the surface like a serpent. "Cold? It's l-l-lovely," he whispered back. "Refreshing. Bracing." He dived back down and stroked underwater away from shore in the cold blackness. Icy, yes, but bearable. For a few minutes anyway. He reached the middle of the lake and treaded water, shaking with the cold. Jake arrived a minute later. As they paused there, teeth chattering, the cloud covering the moon slipped away from it, giving the boys a momentary glimpse of the shoreline. Peter scanned the shore but could make out nothing, and hoped nothing was there to see them. The only sound was the lapping of water, which seemed as oppressive as the clamminess of the night. A deep rumble sounded unexpectedly.

"Thunder," Peter said. "Where there's thunder, there could be lightning, and I'm not in the mood to be electrocuted. Let's get off this lake."

They swam back and exited the water as quietly as they'd entered, taking a few moments to locate their pile of dry clothing.

As they shook off and began dressing, a girl's voice from the brush nearby made them jump.

"Don't worry, I won't look. But you might as well know I'm here."

The two hurriedly finished pulling on their clothing, hopping about, trying to see her. Peter felt around for his headlamp. When they were fully dressed, a flashlight emerged from behind bushes and shone on their faces, blinding them.

Peter ducked her light and directed his beam on her. A girl their age, Hispanic and unsmiling.

"Who are you?" he asked, trying to make his voice sound stern and confident.

"More like, who are you? You're three days early, you know, and past where we were supposed to meet. And where's Ron?"

Peter looked at Jake. Jake looked at Peter. Both tried to shield their eyes from her beam.

"Let me try again. Where's Ron?"

"Who?" Peter answered, studying her as she moved closer and trying to think fast.

"Yeah, sure you don't know Ron. Well then, let me inform you that biking is not permitted in the Pasayten until next month, and I know you didn't just land here by helicopter. Allow me to guess that you've just crossed the border. And since the only bike trail to here is Ron's, and the bikes by your tent match Ron's description — never mind that you're not very good liars — I say you're working for Ron. Okay? It's your turn now."

"You're J.G." Peter finally said.

"Juanita Gonzáles, that's right. Sounds like we're getting somewhere." Her speech carried a hint of a Mexican accent, but she'd probably grown up here, Peter guessed.

"Then where is José?" Peter asked, ignoring Jake's elbow in the ribs.

"Granddad got the flu two days ago. He's camped forty-five minutes back up the trail. He's okay, just weak, so we agreed I'd go ahead to try and finish the trail. I'm heading back tomorrow morning to check on him." She lowered her flashlight, prompting Peter to dim his.

"So you've nearly finished the trail, even with your granddad laid up?" Peter ventured.

Juanita surveyed them coldly. "Yes. I'm a hard worker. So, did Ron send you our money? And are you going to tell me your names?"

"I'm Peter. This is Jake. Ron had to head back to Keremeos for some supplies. He'll be here soon. He didn't give us instructions to pay you. You haven't been in touch with him today?"

Juanita frowned, leveling her gaze at Peter. "You know we don't have phones or radios." After a moment, she lowered her hands from her hips and walked over to a tree, where Peter saw she'd parked her bike. He directed his headlamp onto it. Nice bike. Same brand and model as his, Jake's, Ron's, Hank's, and Laszlo's. He wondered if she, like them, was being kept in the dark about the true nature of the trail. And what her granddad knew. A thunderclap sounded, closer this time.

"Looks like we might finally get rain tonight. Do you want some coffee? My tent is down by the water, next to my raft, which you might have noticed while you were swimming. I built it from some rope and logs. I wanted to get out on the water like you guys just did, but I can't swim. When you first arrived, I hid for a while. Had to decide if you were okay. So, coffee?"

"Uh, so you're here on your own?" Peter asked, still trying to see into the shadows behind Juanita.

"Yes, I'm alone. Follow me." She led the way toward the lake. The boys followed as her words drifted back to them in the darkness. "In the morning, you can show me where to connect our trail with yours. And hopefully Ron will show up to pay us all."

As they arrived at her tent and cookstove, Peter found his tongue. "You bet."

But it seemed Jake wasn't going to let that slide. The minute she'd brewed them some coffee, he worried Peter by starting in with questions.

"Juanita, how did you and your granddad come to be working for Ron, or is it Ron's bosses who hired you?"

Peter watched Juanita eye Jake quizzically.

"Ron has others in on this? He's never mentioned others. He's got a permit for commercial mountain bike tours — I assume you know that — and Granddad just retired from running a mountain biking store in Winthrop. Ron used to buy bikes from us 'cause we had more selection than the Keremeos bike shop. And he liked this area for riding. When he asked

Granddad if he knew anyone who'd be good at helping to build a trail, Granddad signed on."

She tugged on her long black braid and challenged them with her dark brown eyes. "He let me come along because he knows how much I love mountain biking, and I'm good at building trails. He always let me help him with his shop. And I've spent tons of time designing constructions with local riders, even though I prefer urban riding on hard-tails."

"Do you know a Laszlo or Hank?" Jake asked her, making Peter squirm, even if he also wanted to know.

"No. Who are they?" Juanita asked.

"Guys who duped Ron into building this trail for them, when really they're planning to smuggle drugs across the border with it." Although Jake was talking to Juanita, Peter recognized the hidden challenge directed at him.

A loon's cry sliced through the still night as Juanita stared at Jake wide-eyed.

"Says who? Since when?" she finally demanded.

"We overheard them in the woods near where we were camped with Ron," Peter interjected. "We don't know if Ron knows the full score, but we know Ron isn't really the one running the bike tours. He told us that. He thinks his friends are."

"Friends? But he told Granddad and me he was starting up a tour company. With a license," she emphasized. "Why wouldn't he have said if it was for someone else?"

"To protect us," Peter declared, holding up a hand as Jake leaned forward to interrupt. "He may have had a sense that not everything was aboveboard. He was protecting us, just in case his instincts were right that the friends who had hired him to build the trail weren't giving him the full story."

"Or is he in with them, if they're actually doing what you say they're doing?" Juanita pressed. "I can't believe that, knowing Ron. I used to bike with him and his sister when they came to visit sometimes, before she had her baby. But I have to ask why you're so sure his friends are dishonest and he's not."

"Because," Peter declared, again cutting Jake off, "he helped us get away from his friends when they decided we knew too much and came after us with a knife. And because we saw they'd beaten him up. And because, well, we just know Ron too well." Peter's eyes sought Jake's, which grew warmer. The three discussed the details of the chase and speculated on where Ron might be now, and in what condition.

"Why would Ron get himself tangled up with people he's not sure about?" Juanita wondered aloud.

"For his sister," Jake spoke up.

"Oh, yeah," Juanita said, placing her now empty coffee cup on the ground. "He did say he was helping her buy her house. He's something around her, you know. Never met a brother so into looking after a sister."

Peter turned to catch the glow on Jake's face. Not unlike Jake and Alyson, it suddenly occurred to him. He turned back to Juanita. "Do you have any brothers or sisters?"

The girl flipped her braid over her shoulder roughly. "No. My parents were killed in a car accident when I was six. Granddad's from Mexico originally but he's raised me here in the States. But look," Juanita said, dark eyes narrowing, "I'm worried about Ron. If some goons have got him and are looking to use our trail for something illegal, we'd better get this to the police. We'll ride out to Granddad's tent first thing tomorrow morning, okay? Then we'll follow the trail out to Winthrop. I'd have gone back to Granddad this evening, but I was totally bushed. Then you guys showed up. Anyway, I'm not going to do it in the dark tonight."

"Agreed," Peter said, echoed by Jake. "Juanita, do you have any food that's not pepperoni sticks?"

13   Storm

Jake tossed and turned on top of his sleeping bag in the humid night, coming fully awake whenever thunder boomed or flashes of lightning lit up the walls of the tent. The tent glowed eerily before being plunged into darkness again. During wakeful moments, Jake worried. First he worried that Juanita might have lied about not knowing Hank and Laszlo. Maybe she was even in with them, and not with Ron? But that was highly unlikely; she seemed totally honest. Too bad Ron had no phone contact with her and her granddad, but Laszlo and Hank had probably forbidden it for fear that messages between the teams might be intercepted by border patrols.

Jake also worried about Ron. Had Ron been injured badly before Laszlo chased the boys? Or had he gotten away? Had Hank returned to camp and persuaded Ron to help pull Laszlo out of the creek, maybe on a stretcher they rigged up? He must have. Hank couldn't have done it on his own, especially if he was injured himself. Finally, Jake wondered how long it would take Juanita's trail to get them to Winthrop.

The rain never came, and the dry lightning storm continued well into the night. Once, Jake was awakened by the thundering of hooves. Was he dreaming, or had a deer just galloped by? Despite the bouts of wakefulness, Jake had managed to fall asleep when an explosion ripped him from his slumber. He and Peter sat straight up, frightened and disoriented. Heart pounding, Jake was the first one to scramble up to unzip the tent door.

"Sounded like a gunshot," he whispered, peering into the darkness.

"It did," Peter agreed, his voice unsteady.

They listened but could hear only the wind, which had picked up. Branches creaked and gusts howled. The sides of their tent rippled and puffed like labored breathing. Forest debris blew along the ground outside like herds of scurrying mice. Jake took a deep breath. The night air smelled strange, but his mind was still too groggy to determine in what way.

"Listen," Peter whispered. Jake strained his ears. He registered two sounds: a faint crackling noise and feet padding toward them in a hurry. His body tensed.

Should he cower in the corner of the tent, dash out boldly, or search for something he could use as a weapon?

"Jake, Peter," they heard Juanita's voice call. He relaxed a little. "Come help!"

They bounded out of the tent and crashed into each other in an effort to sprint toward her voice, which came from somewhere along the creek behind their tent. Now the distinct smell of smoke stung Jake's nostrils. The crackling noise made sense.

"Fire!" Juanita yelled. "Get water!" The two reached for their water bottles, feeling foolish as they realized how little that was going to help, and scanned the forest around them. Had he not been looking in the direction of Juanita's voice, Jake wouldn't have seen it immediately: a fallen tree branch, no more than six feet long, lying halfway across the creek bed and dancing with small orange flames. It was a branch from the very tree against which they'd parked their bikes, a long stone's throw from their tent.

Jake sprinted toward the silhouette of Juanita dipping a large cooking pot of water into the creek and pouring it over the flames as Peter reached into their tent for his headlamp.

"Sssssst" came the sound of Juanita's dousing. Jake waded into the creek and scooped water up into his water bottle, then dumped it onto the portion of the branch that was still on fire. As Peter did the same, Jake looked about. The forest was "as dry as a tinderbox," an expression he remembered Ron using the first day of the trip. They were lucky the lightning had downed just this one branch, which had formed half the upper "Y" of a large tree. They were also lucky that most of it had fallen in the creek bed behind it, and that Juanita had gotten there so quickly with her cooking pot. He and Peter had nothing that could hold water except their water bottles.

Soon, they had every hot spot on the branch saturated with water.

"One more dousing just to be sure," Jake suggested, as Peter aimed his headlamp on the blackened hunk of tree, then peered up the trunk from which it had fallen. The boys and Juanita scanned the entire forest around them, looking for further signs of lightning strikes.

"No more that I can see," Peter said, echoing Jake's thoughts. "Close one. We're lucky you got here in time," he said, nodding to Juanita.

"*No problemo,*" she said as she poured one more potful along it like a farmer filling a feeding trough. "I couldn't sleep, what with the heat and noise and lightning flashes. I was looking up here when it hit. Sounded like a cannon going off, and it lit up like a fireball as it dropped. Good thing it was just half the tree, and that it split off cleanly like this. And thank goodness it fell in the creek, especially since your bikes are parked this side of it."

"They're fine. I checked them," Peter spoke up.

"We couldn't have done much if it had burned upward, and then spread," Juanita observed. She sank to the ground, clearly spent from her efforts. Jake felt exhaustion creep into his own body. He shone his headlamp on his watch: "Two o'clock. It's going to be a job getting back to sleep after this."

"Not for me," Juanita said, yawning, pulling herself up, and nodding at them dismissively. "See you in the morning." Then she was gone, swallowed by the darkness like a forest pixie.

Jake looked at Peter, who was kicking the damp log. His flashlight framed wet ashes dropping into the dark creek.

"Never liked the smell of smoke," Peter commented, wrinkling his nose. "Glad we're not too close to it. I know I can get back to sleep, especially since it's stopped thundering and lightning. Better yet, we have no one to kick us out of bed in the morning."

The last comment, far from helping Jake settle back to sleep once they'd crawled back into their tent, brought on the same confused sadness and fear he'd been battling ever since those goons had appeared. Ron had risked his life to help Jake get away, after all.

Where was he now? Should they have gone back to find out? But Jake's head throbbed just thinking about the muddle of events. Long after Peter's breathing indicated he was fast asleep, Jake lay there, worrying, wondering, feeling a sense of loss. It took him hours to clear his mind enough to begin to drift off to sleep, and that was shattered by the sound of a plane flying low overhead.

"What the ..." Peter grumbled, rolling over and pulling a portion of his sleeping bag over his head. "What next?!"

Two minutes later, Peter was snoring, as if *that* was going to help Jake drop off. But he might as well not even have tried, because several more planes flew over, or the same one back and forth, between four and five o'clock in the morning.

Jake's eyelids hurt from the effort of trying to sleep. And then he was gone, pulled into unconsciousness and troubled dreams by total exhaustion.

When he awoke, it felt late. The tent sides were billowing like sails in a storm. The wind had really picked up. He looked at his watch: ten o'clock. He was about to shake Peter awake when he thought, "Why? What's to get up for?"

As the events of the night came back to him, his senses went on high alert. Crackling! The smell of smoke! He jumped up and shook Peter.

"Peter, Peter, get up! I think the forest is on fire."

Peter's eyes opened wide. The two scrambled out of the tent for the second time that day and stared, horrified. The trunk of the tree whose branch they had doused so carefully last night was lit up like a torch. They backed up instinctively, the tent between them and the tree trunk.

"Ohmigod, I think it's going to set this whole place on fire," Jake said. They watched as the tree spilled smoking chunks onto the ground, sparking flames that raced off in every direction like fuses.

"Our tent! Our bikes!" Jake shouted into the wind, backing up more as a line of flames shot toward his boot-clad feet. But before he could sprint toward the bikes, he felt Peter's arm jerk him in the opposite direction.

"Too late. Run for the lake. *Now.*"

Jake looked to Peter, then to their tent in disbelief. Abandon their bikes and gear? But Peter was right. Fire had reached their tent already and was licking at the forest floor beneath their feet, snaking in every direction, rapidly closing off their options.

The boys dashed down to the lake, leaping over burning twigs and dry logs. With trembling hands, they shook Juanita's tent, relieved when she shouted, "What?"

Glancing back at what was fast becoming a wall of

fire, the boys dragged Juanita out before she was fully awake and pointed up the slope.

"Whaaa?" she said, rubbing her eyes, pulling on her boots, and coughing from the smoke. As they stood there in shock, their backs to the lake, Jake looked left, right, and center. Directly up the north slope, where they'd been camped, the wind-driven blaze was lighting up the forest like a gasoline-drenched bonfire. To the east, a stony ridge curved down from the sheer treed cliffs behind the lake. To the west, the forest remained green and untouched, stretching gently away from the lake. It offered a possible escape route, as long as the fire didn't spread there.

Jake turned and studied the lake. It was small, and he knew it to be deadly cold. No more than 300 yards across. He'd heard of forest fires jumping small lakes in high winds like this. And they'd die of hypothermia in no time if they were forced in. But what else could they do?

"My grandfather!" Juanita suddenly shrieked and sprinted to her bike. As she pointed it west, Jake and Peter bolted after her.

"Let go! Get off!" she screamed, beating at their hands as they held her bike.

"You can't outride a forest fire in winds like this," Jake said as firmly as he dared, his forehead all but touching hers as he leaned over her handlebars and faced her down. "We have to stay by the lake."

"*You* stay by the lake! You're not in charge of me. Let go now or you'll be sorry," she said, eyes flashing, hands rolling into fists. Jake was so taken aback by her rage that he let go for a split second. That's when she heaved her elbow backward into Peter's gut and raised a foot to kick him hard in his groin. She sprinted away before Jake could decide whether to wrestle her or tend to Peter, who was writhing on the ground. She was heading west for the green crescent of blowing trees, ignoring the inferno on her right.

"Can't believe it," Peter huffed. "She's nuts. We were trying to help her."

"She'll be back," Jake predicted, "if she's lucky."

Peter shrugged. "Or maybe she *will* make it out. It's up to the winds, when and how they change direction. We're lucky we're downhill and downwind of the fire right now."

"Forget her. We need a plan. And I don't think our plan is going to involve her trail, even though we know where it is now," Jake said.

They watched Juanita disappear into the trees, then turned to survey the blaze, which seemed more intent on spreading uphill to the north than marching downhill to force them into the lake. Squinting up toward their campsite, Jake sucked in his breath as he saw that space totally engulfed in flames. He imagined their bikes' rubber tires melting, boiling, and disintegrating. He imagined the acrid smell that would make. He wiped perspiration off his forehead as the flames leaped higher, consuming the trees in a crazed frenzy. The crackling and sparks, the black, billowing smoke, and the way flaming branches fell softly in slow motion, awed Jake. He was mesmerized by the power and speed with which the raging flames moved from one area to the next. His skin turned to goosebumps as one giant tree crashed near their former campsite. He felt Peter's hand rest on his shoulder.

14   Refuge

"A plan, you said. Let's make a plan."

Jake wondered how long he and Peter had stood entranced by the show. Yes, he had to force himself to action, tear his smarting eyes away from the terrible yet strangely compelling blaze. The heat was beginning to draw beads of sweat on his body. The smoke, though mostly billowing in the opposite direction, was irritating his nose and throat. He turned around to look at the lake. Remembered, again, that wind-driven forest fires can jump right over lakes. Peter followed his gaze.

"The raft!" they exclaimed together as their eyes locked on Juanita's handmade craft. It was small and very roughly laced together with a short length of climbing rope, but it looked seaworthy enough for their purposes. Jake rifled through Juanita's campsite, grabbing a water bottle and some chocolate bars. He and Peter hadn't eaten a full meal for more than a day, yet hunger hadn't hit him until now, just from spotting Juanita's food supplies. Peter joined him in opening containers.

"Rice. Coffee. Beans. Moldy burrito shells. Gross. Useless. Okay, here we go. Peanut butter. Attagirl. I'll take that and a spoon; you grab water. Fire's closer, Jake. The wind is turning. We're going to have to back into that lake soon."

Jake felt panic well up in his chest. He could feel the heat like a furnace blast now. He wasn't keen to test Juanita's jury-rigged jumble of logs, but he'd seen how fast the fire could move already and knew Peter was right. The wind was shifting. The wall of fire was creeping downhill. He glanced at the place they'd last seen Juanita. It was still clear, treetops swaying as if trying to bewitch the fire, or perhaps performing the last rites for the trees' own coming funeral. His eyes stung from the ash, heat, and smoke. He backed up until his boot heels were touching the lake.

"It's time," Peter said, removing his boots and crawling onto the craft with Juanita's peanut butter, a water bottle, and a broad stick the size of a paddle. The corner nearest the shore promptly dipped into the water, forcing Peter to stretch out his hands and push the far side down. Sitting gingerly in the middle, pulling his boots (water bottle in one, peanut butter jar in the other) into his lap, he held his arm out to Jake. Reluctantly, Jake unlaced his boots, tossed them to Peter, and waded a few steps toward the raft.

"How long do you think we'll have to wait it out?" he asked.

"Whatever it takes. Never done this before," Peter replied, taking Jake's hand and pulling him aboard. They almost flipped right then and there, but with a little scrambling, they managed to spread the load evenly enough to gain stability. Peter stuck his stick into the mud and pushed the raft out into deeper water, slowly. It wobbled, tilted, spun, and wet their bottoms through the cracks.

As they drifted toward the lake's center, Jake and Peter watched the shore succumb to flames. Just one lightning strike to one tree near their tent nine hours ago had started all this. Now massive flames roared for miles on one broad side of the lake, like a regiment in arch formation closing in. Yet still, Juanita's route remained unsinged, biding its time like a self-declared neutral zone between countries engaged in war. Likewise, the cliff behind the lake and the stone ridge to one side watched, sentry to the rampant destruction.

More to occupy themselves than to satiate their hunger, the two took turns plunging the spoon into the peanut butter. It felt very surreal, Jake thought, to be picnicking cross-legged on an unstable raft in the middle of a glacial green lake on a windy morning, orange flames crackling and advancing to the northern edge of their shore.

They watched in sober silence as the fire reached Juanita's billowing tent and it burst into flames. Jake's mind flashed back to their camp up in Cathedral Park. Would this fire reach there? They'd brought nothing away but sleeping bags, tent, headlamps, and snack food, now all consumed by the fire. His jar with Alyson's butterflies was up there. Oh well. And Ron? Was he lying in camp injured and helpless? Or had he, Hank, and Laszlo somehow escaped? Would the fire catch them?

"What do people do if they're caught by a forest fire without a lake or river to climb into?" Jake wondered aloud, throat tight.

"They try to hide in a gully, or they bury themselves in dirt, face down. They breathe through wet clothing, if they can, and hope the fire won't steal their oxygen before it passes over. Or if they have time, they burn a patch of grass before the fire reaches them, to give them some cooled scorched earth to lie down on. Then they hope the flames won't leap over and catch them on fire."

Both boys were quiet for a moment. "My grandfather told me this stuff," Peter added. He cupped his hands and dipped them into the lake, then lifted and dribbled the water over their raft. "I'm wetting it down, just in case," he said. Jake didn't bother to point out that the leaky raft was already plenty wet. Peter rambled on. "Did you know that firefighters carry special fireproof tents to wrap around themselves if they get caught out? But they sometimes smother inside them."

Jake shuddered.

"Ten o'clock. Should have known," said Peter. Since it was now past eleven, Jake turned to him quizzically.

"Firefighters call it the ten a.m. concept. They dread it. That's when humidity drops, temperatures rise, and winds pick up all at the same time. It turns smoldering bits into flames. That's when most wildfires start, especially after dry lightning storms."

"Then why aren't there any firefighters here?" Jake asked bitterly.

"Who knows how many other blazes are going?" Peter replied, trailing his stick in the water. "But we did hear planes this morning, didn't we? I was mostly asleep."

"Yeah, just as it was getting light," Jake said.

"Forest Service doing infrared scans," Peter said. "They have a big board at their headquarters that uses global positioning scanning — GPS — to show each lightning strike. They send out planes that fly over those areas to see if any strikes pop up as smoke."

"So where *are* the smokejumpers and fire crews and planes?" Jake pressed in exasperation. So much of the forest was disappearing by the hour.

Peter looked up and studied the hazy sky. "They'll be here," he said with assurance, "and then we'll get a ride out by helicopter. They may even be on the ground battling their way toward us now."

"What about Juanita? What about Ron?" Jake couldn't stand holding those worries back any more.

Peter shifted his gaze to the north, studied the Canadian peaks through billows of black smoke.

"Ron's a survivor, remember? He can take care of himself, Jake. We've seen that more than once. No thug or fire is going to snuff him. He has as many lives as two cats." He gave Jake's shoulder a squeeze, almost as if he understood Jake's turmoil. Jake didn't move, didn't look at Peter, but let the calm of that touch radiate from his shoulder to the rest of his body. Ron was okay, and the fire wouldn't touch him. Jake believed Peter.

"As for Juanita ..." Peter began, but he was interrupted by a scream from somewhere behind them. The two swung around to see a figure on the thirty-foot-high cliff, a small figure on a bike, surrounded by flames. When had the fire reached around behind the lake? Jake grabbed the paddle-stick from Peter and began splashing to move the raft closer to the cliff.

"Jump!" he shouted at Juanita. In the same instant, he remembered that she had built the raft because she couldn't swim.

She dropped her bike beside her, shuffled from one foot to another, arms wrapped around her chest, eyes wide, head jerking from the lake to the fire behind her.

"Jump!" Jake urged again. "We'll get you. We know you can't swim."

A gust of wind blew burning debris off the clifftop and into the water. The next gust brought a clump of burning moss down on Juanita's hair, which prompted a new scream. She leaped off the cliff, hands slapping her head.

The raft was still several yards from where Juanita plunged in. Jake dived in so fast after her that he had no time to register a single thought. The cold took his breath away, but he was totally focused on reaching Juanita's panicked and flailing body. He remembered to approach her from behind and to place his arm around her neck so she couldn't clutch him and pull him under.

"Relax," he instructed her through chattering teeth. "Relax and trust me. Don't fight or I can't help you. We're going to get you back to the raft."

She stopped struggling, although her body remained stiff. Her hands clenched his elbow as he drew her through wind-tossed water toward the raft. Peter was waiting there to draw her up, when a roar sounded from shore. They turned to see a great gust of wind throw a wall of fire toward them.

"Dive!" Peter shouted as he slid off the raft head-first. Jake, heart thumping, took a deep breath, placed his hands on Juanita's shoulders, and pushed her down gently. He was amazed she didn't resist. Underwater, he placed his hands on top of hers and guided them to the underside of the raft, where she could get a grip. He couldn't believe she was cooperating. If she'd fought his efforts to get her to duck underwater, the blowtorch from shore would surely have burned her head. Jake kept both his hands in contact with hers, hoping that would calm her, and felt Peter's hand reach out to join theirs. They were all under the raft, numb with cold and fear, counting until their lungs were ready to burst, hoping the fire's jump across the lake would be finished by the time they surfaced.

Still clutching Juanita, Jake popped up long enough to catch a breath, made sure Juanita did the same, and went back down for another count, just to be certain. The cold made it difficult to hold his breath. It seemed to press on his body from both sides. They'd never have lasted long in this lake without the raft, he realized.

When he came up the next time, the danger had passed. But something else had also passed: a helicopter was disappearing to the west. Jake looked at Peter, saw him studying it too.

"It'll be back," Peter said as he slung a leg up on the raft and positioned himself to help pull Juanita up. Shivering uncontrollably, Juanita let the two of them help her out of the water. The extra weight on the tiny raft sank it well into the water, but it remained afloat. Juanita's eyes were large as she lay sprawled and wet, shivering.

"Th-thanks," she mumbled. "And s-s-sorry about before."

Peter hesitated before replying, "Apologies accepted. Guess it makes sense you were worried about your granddad. Did you find him? Where is he?"

Jake decided to change the subject so Juanita wouldn't feel a need to talk about her granddad. "It's either too hot or too cold around here. Hot and cold seem to be our only choices. Look at our boots, Peter. Toasted lightly at the top." He gazed at the slightly scorched boots, then at the blackened shoreline, now a mess of charred and still burning logs. Only hours before, this had been a beautiful forest. Where were the mule deer, the mountain sheep, the chipmunks, pikas, and squirrels now? Had they known when and where to run?

"My granddad wasn't there," Juanita spoke in a choked voice. They turned to her. "He wasn't anywhere around camp. The tent and supplies were, but not him."

"Were you camped somewhere exposed? A hill or anything? Maybe he got picked up by helicopter," Peter suggested gently.

She looked at Peter hopefully. "Yes, a bare hill. Do you think?"

"Yes, and he knows where you are. So they'll find us soon. That helicopter was probably them looking for us. Are you hungry? If you don't mind sharing a spoon, we haven't finished off all your peanut butter."

She gawked at him as he produced the jar from inside one of his scorched boots. Finally, a smile tugged at her face, softening her otherwise tough features.

"*Gracias*," she said, digging in with the spoon.

15   A Lift

"**S**o much for all our hard trail-building," Juanita said at length. They had been sitting tensely on the raft, hardly daring to move for fear of tipping it. Peter watched the girl's eyes survey the burning trees through which she had biked only hours before. He recalled her jump off the cliff into the lake. Must have been terrifying for someone who couldn't swim, especially when her hair nearly caught fire. She was still scared sitting on this tippy raft, he could tell. But she was hiding it well.

"Yup, a week of trail-building down the drain. But if we're right that no permit was ever going to come through and it was designed for drug-smuggling bike couriers, maybe it's just fate," Peter commented.

"Funny, Granddad and I never questioned the permit thing. Do you think any of us will get paid now? And will we get into trouble?"

"We might not get paid," Jake spoke up, "but we shouldn't get in trouble because we didn't know about the permit not being through, or the drug stuff."

"And Ron?" Juanita's question hung heavily in the air.

Peter watched Jake wring his hands as his buddy stared north. "I think," Peter began, "that if Ron turns in Laszlo and Hank, and cooperates with police, they won't charge him. But they'll give him a pretty hard time."

"We'll help the police understand that Ron wasn't part of it," Juanita insisted. "You guys are the best witnesses for that."

Peter looked at Jake, who looked at Peter, jaw set.

"That's true," Peter agreed. "You and your grandfather will get questioned, too."

"All we have to do is be honest," she asserted.

Peter and Jake nodded soberly.

"Jake, I owe you an apology for not trusting Ron," Peter said softly. He was surprised as Jake shook his head.

"No, I should apologize for being so stubborn. You were weighing things more carefully, making our safety the highest priority. My stubbornness ended up being the thing that got us into trouble. I should never have gotten mad at you where Laszlo and Hank could hear us. Guess I had what they call blind loyalty.

Could've turned out pretty badly if you hadn't put together a Plan B."

"You mean having a backpack ready to go? And the way I stayed at the edge of the campsite?" Peter asked.

Jake nodded.

"You know, after I spied on you," she said, wringing water from her wet braid, "I had a plan for getting away from you two if my instincts told me not to trust you. But I figured I'd approach you first, and go with my intuition."

Jake and Peter peered at her. "Guess we passed the test?" Jake asked.

Juanita smiled. "Guess so."

The three went quiet for a while, then lifted their heads as a plane's drone sounded.

"Rescue time," Peter declared, resisting the urge to kneel and wave as he felt the raft wobble beneath him. He was elated as the plane dipped lower and sped directly toward them, and he gave his raft-mates a thumbs-up as it powered directly overhead and slowed. But he was appalled as he saw it release a bright plume of red dust, which fell like a shower on the burning trees along the cliff. As the plane lifted away, the three started coughing and rubbing their eyes.

"Fire retardant!" Peter cried in dismay, eyes closed tightly and hands trying to beat it off his wet shirt and hair.

"It stings!" Peter heard Jake's voice. Peter's hands found the edge of the raft and he plunged his entire head in, using his hands to rinse the annoying chemicals out of his hair and face. When he came up again, he felt Juanita grab his back. "You almost tipped us in, Peter! Stop moving around like that."

He nodded and watched as she and Jake followed his actions, moving much more cautiously to wash their faces. Just then, the sky seemed to explode with sound. One, then two, helicopters appeared, plying the air over the forest fire. One moved to hover above the lake. Peter looked up to see a face lean out. An arm appeared next, jabbing in the direction of the stony ridge on the east edge of the lake. The flames beside the natural rock platform had died down considerably since the fire had jumped over the lake and the plane had dropped a cloud of chemicals.

Peter picked up the paddle and started to stroke the water. With three bodies on board, however, the craft was as unwilling to move as a stubborn pack-donkey. Jake lay on his stomach and used an arm as a paddle to add force to Peter's efforts as Juanita sat stock-still in the center, wide-eyed, fingers clinging tightly to the logs. The helicopter had moved to the ridge now and was touching down. A woman in a bright orange jumpsuit stepped out of the passenger seat. Carrying a rope coiled in her hand, she ducked and ran to the lake's edge, sliding down the last of the steep embankment.

Peter cursed as the raft continued to move at a snail's pace. He wasn't surprised when Jake spoke up.

"I'll swim over there. That'll ease the weight on here," he said. And off he slid like a seal, stroking to shore in a burst of energy. Now Juanita, biting her lower lip, took Jake's place, lying full-length and lending her arm to the slow but steady forward movement. When they were twenty-five feet from shore, the orange-suited firefighter tossed Peter an end of her rope. He caught it, tied it around some of the log ends, and let the woman and Jake haul the raft in as Juanita gripped its sides.

The firefighter smiled as they landed and extended her hand to Juanita first. "Hi, I'm Laura Peck. And that's our pilot Phillip. We weren't expecting three of you, just one. Your grandfather is safe back at headquarters, Juanita. I'm assuming you're Juanita."

Juanita nodded as a smile lit her face.

"Where did you boys come from? And was there anyone else in your party?"

"It's a long story," Peter replied, "but it's just us."

"Okay, well, I want to hear that long story, but for now I'm just glad we found you. Now up to the helicopter, and keep your head low as you board."

As if we've never been in a helicopter, Peter

thought with a smile, thinking back to a certain heli-snowboarding and skiing adventure. He raced behind Juanita and Jake as the firefighter, a first-aid pack and fire shelter strapped to her waist, followed behind.

But he halted as his eyes spotted something beneath a scorched tree at the edge of the rocky ground a few yards away. Without asking Laura for permission, he detoured a few long strides and knelt to pick it up: a bird's nest, three of its four eggs still intact. He clutched it to his chest and met the eyes of the firefighter, who was waving him sternly toward the waiting chopper. He squeezed into the back seat beside Jake and Juanita and breathed freely when their rescuer slammed the helicopter door shut and climbed into the front. Placing the nest gently in his lap to curious looks from all aboard, he strapped on his seatbelt and donned headphones as the pilot, not losing a minute, lifted off.

What a view. For the first time, Peter took in the full swath of destruction and noted an army of orange-suited firefighters creating a long trench as a fire break due west of where their fire had started. He noticed they were working in pairs, one hacking at the ground with a tool that had an ax head at one end and a grubbing blade on the other, and the other shoveling dirt onto stray flames.

Pulaskis. That's what those tools are called, Peter

thought, remembering that his grandpa had one hanging on his den wall. Where had these crews come from, and when? He looked further to the east, only to see at least three other, smaller fires, not yet joined together. These were being tended by planes dropping fire retardant and yet more crews outfitted with hoses and ground machinery. The hoses were pulling water from the creek Jake and Peter had cycled down. Crews with more hoses had just reached their lake. All the fires looked nearly under control. To the south and far north, untouched greenery stretched away, as pristine as all the forest had been just twenty-four hours ago, and hopefully safe from harm today, if the crews had their way.

"Like I said, Juanita, your grandfather is at the Forest Service headquarters in Winthrop, which is where we're headed," Laura's voice crackled through the earphones. "We picked him up around eleven when we were dropping fire crews. Now, I want to hear that story about what you boys were doing in that forest?"

"I don't even know where to begin," Peter said. Laura turned her head to study him, and he plunged in. "Jake and I were in Cathedral Park on the Canadian side of the border when some drug smugglers started chasing us ..."

"One had a knife," Jake cut in.

"And they escaped by hiding, then riding down the creek bed," Juanita said excitedly.

"After one guy got badly hurt, maybe both did ..."

"And then we ran into Juanita here, and she woke us up when lightning struck the tree next to our tent ..."

"Hold on, hold on," Laura protested, holding her hand up as they all began speaking at once. "Drug smugglers? And you crossed the border to here? You're not having me on? This is a major incident to report if you're telling me the truth."

"The truth and nothing but the truth," Jake said. "Like Peter said, it's a long story. Has the fire gone north across the border?"

"No, but Canadian officials are on full alert."

"We can tell you the whole story when we get to headquarters."

"Yes, the drug-smuggling story *and* the way you escaped from the fire." Laura said. "You did exactly the right thing getting onto the lake without getting into it, which would have made you hypothermic. Who made the raft?"

The boys pointed at Juanita, who smiled.

Peter looked down at his bird's nest and noticed that the vibrations of the helicopter were inflicting some tiny cracks in one of the eggs.

Twenty-five minutes later, the helicopter hovered

over a landing pad beside some squat green buildings topped by a tower with antennas rising high above it. As the pilot cut the throttle, he turned around and extended a hand to each of the three in turn. "Laura will see you into headquarters. Move along, kids; we've got fire crews waiting to be transported."

"Thank you," Peter's voice echoed Jake's and Juanita's as he turned to see a lineup of orange-suited men and women, each carrying Pulaskis, shovels, chainsaws, and metal cans with long nozzles. Those, Peter knew, were drip torches to pour out fuel in a controlled manner. The firefighters also wore little waist packs just like Laura Peck's. They smiled as he saluted them, one hand still cupped around his bird's nest. He watched as Juanita ran to a fit-looking, gray-haired man coming out of the building and noticed Laura duck into headquarters.

"*Abuelito!*" Juanita cried as she threw herself into the man's arms.

Peter and Jake stood back politely as the two embraced and exchanged some fast-paced Spanish. Then the boys moved forward with hands extended as Juanita's grandfather pulled away to greet them.

"Ah, the other half of our team minus Ron," he said. "Juanita here assures me that Ron wasn't with you in the Pasayten Wilderness and that the fire hasn't spread up to Canada. I am so happy Ron is safe. She says she'll tell me the story of your escape this afternoon, but I understand you took part in her rescue and I want to thank you."

Peter cast a sideways glance at Jake, who looked anxious at the mention of Ron's name. Sure, they knew the fire hadn't spread to Cathedral Park, but they still had no way of knowing if Ron had survived his wrestling match with Laszlo. "*No problemo,*" Peter said with a sympathetic nod to Jake and a wink at Juanita.

"I should never have let her go ahead alone …"

"Oh, Granddad, it's me who shouldn't have left you alone," Juanita said, hugging him again. "I'm so glad you got rescued."

"And I can't tell you how relieved I was when I heard you had been lifted out," he said, face broken into worry lines. "But here come some officials looking to debrief us, judging by those clipboards and badges."

Peter turned to nod at Laura, who was leading two uniformed rangers. "Ummm, before we start," he said, "can I borrow a quarter for the phone booth? It's a local call, to my grandpa."

One of the Forest Service men laughed. "I think we can do better than that. I think we can offer you free use of a phone, some dry clothes, and cups of coffee. But besides all those and a conference with us, you seem to need somewhere warm to finish hatching those birds. Lucky for you we have a naturalist on duty."

Peter looked down. Sure enough, a baby bird had pecked its way halfway out of one of his eggs. The tiny creature moved its wet, scrawny neck to peer up at him.

"No worries," he said, speaking to both the Forest Service official and the bird.

16　Winthrop

Jake could definitely handle being at Peter's grandparents' house for a few days. Today was Tuesday, three days since they'd been lifted out by helicopter, and now that his mom knew they were safe and in good hands, he could relax and enjoy the way Peter's grandmother, Trish Montpetit, fussed over them. There were the big, home-cooked meals she sometimes delivered by tray to the basement games room, where the boys were spending tons of time on video games, the super-sized television screen, the foosball or pool tables. Then there was the guestroom half the size of Jake's Chilliwack bungalow. And the new clothes that Mrs. Montpetit had bought them, since they'd arrived with nothing but the clothes on their backs.

He and Peter could sleep in as long as they liked, and loll around the deck chairs on the back patio with lemonades when they weren't exploring the town and museums of Winthrop, with its fun, frontier-look facades and rustic boardwalks down Main Street.

The only thing they were missing, Jake reflected as he practiced putting the eight-ball into a corner pocket on the pool table, was news of Ron, which Forest Service headquarters, working with local police, promised to deliver them "after we complete our investigation." Part of the investigation, of course, had involved questioning the boys and Juanita over several sessions, including much of yesterday. Jake and Peter had tried phoning Ron's house a couple of times, but there had been no answer. Jake had a feeling the rangers and police knew more than they were letting on about where and how Ron was.

"Hey there." Peter's grandfather, Paul Montpetit, interrupted his train of thought as he descended the basement steps. Jake smiled at the tall, husky man with a moustache that curled neatly at the ends like an admiral's. "Peter's upstairs rarin' to go to the Smokejumper Base before it closes in an hour. Coming with us?"

"You bet. Wouldn't miss it for the world," Jake agreed. He took the stairs two at a time as Mr. Montpetit, chuckling, kept pace behind him.

"Heard from the Forest Service officials yet?" Jake called out.

"Not yet, but they'll call soon, I'm sure," Mr. Montpetit replied. "Especially if you stop asking every hour."

Within ten minutes, the three were at the North Cascades Smokejumper Base and trailing the end of the afternoon's last public tour. As Jake and Mr. Monpetit passed a display of historical black-and-white photographs depicting the country's first smokejumpers in the early 1940s, Jake pointed to one.

"That's you!" he guessed, spotting a lean young man with the same trim moustache in a lineup of new recruits. "You look a little like Peter, except for the moustache."

"Hmmm, I'll take that as a compliment," Mr. Montpetit laughed, resting a hand on his grandson's shoulder.

"Did you really parachute 3,000 feet out of planes almost into fires?"

"That was our job, to attack small wildland fires in remote areas before they got out of control. We were trained to suit up and board the plane within ten minutes."

"Whoa, get a load of this funny-looking old jump-suit," Peter said, touching a two-piece, felt-padded Kevlar uniform on a mannequin. "What's with the big pocket on one trouser leg and the wire mesh on the football helmet?"

"The pocket held rope that we used to let ourselves down from trees when we didn't land on the ground," Mr. Montpetit replied with a grin. "The helmet was to protect us when we slammed into rocks or trees during the descent. The Kevlar also helped protect us from the heat of the fire. And as you can see, we wore logging boots, ankle braces, and a special belt to protect our backs."

"Must've weighed a ton."

"Eighty pounds by the time you added the gear we jumped with," Mr. Montpetit confirmed. "Then our planes would drop 100-pound fireboxes of tools, food, and water by parachute to last us forty-eight hours. We basically made up the job as we went back then — we just kept improving gear and training."

"It had to be way riskier in the old days," Peter pressed, "without special fireproof tents and all."

"Maybe, but today's wildfire fighters aren't any less brave or dedicated, and we still lose some from time to time," he responded soberly.

"Did you ever get caught out?" Jake asked. "Ever get trapped somewhere?"

"Had to crawl into a stream once, as Peter has heard many a time," Mr. Montpetit replied. "But it wasn't very windy, so the fire never leaped over, like it went over your lake. That means you've survived worse than me, and handled it very well indeed," he said, clapping them on their backs.

"Doesn't make me want to be a smokejumper," Peter admitted.

"Well, with all the roads cut into forests now, and all the technical equipment, smokejumpers aren't needed as much today," Mr. Montpetit said, sounding wistful to Peter's ears. "It's easier to get crews and equipment in faster. On the other hand, there are more people and properties to save."

"But you'll always be famous for being one of the first," Peter enthused. "Hey, the tour has gotten way ahead of us. Let's go see the jumper plane and the practice jumps and the modern cargo boxes —"

He was cut off by the ringing of Mr. Montpetit's cellphone.

"Paul Montpetit. Uh-huh. I see. Well, absolutely. I'll have them up there in a jiffy." He pocketed his cellphone.

"Sorry, guys, we'll have to come back here another day."

"What? Who was it?" Peter demanded.

"Was it Ron?" Jake pressed.

"Into the car, boys. We're off to the Forest Service headquarters to meet Juanita and some folks keen to talk to you."

Shortly before they pulled into the now familiar

headquarters, Jake and Peter managed to get the truth out of Peter's smiling grandfather: A television crew from Seattle wanted to interview the boys and Juanita about their dramatic escape from the fire.

As they pulled into the parking lot, they saw Juanita coming down a hill on a mountain bike and speeding toward a double set of stairs on the grounds. Off the upper landing she flew, right over the first set of steps and middle landing, to land on the lower steps before pulling up neatly beside some startled-looking rangers.

Jake tried not to stare at her. She was dressed in a clingy red top and shorts that showed off her slim, athletic build. Her dark hair, instead of hanging in a braid down her back, was loose and curly beneath her helmet. She looked happy and carefree, such a contrast to the tense girl who'd clutched the raft sides for hours, or the tough girl who had kneed Peter to get to her grandfather. Her bike was identical to the one Ron had been riding; her father obviously had connections to scare her up another so quickly. And Jake had a feeling she was going to give them a run for their money on the urban biking around Winthrop they'd agreed to tomorrow.

"Hi, Jake and Peter," she called out as she spotted them emerging from the car.

That prompted a man and woman stepping out of

a slick van to look their way and approach with hands extended.

"So you're the youths who escaped the fire," the man said. "I'm Christopher Seaman from KOMO-TV News in Seattle, and this is my camerawoman, Meredith. So glad to meet you, and we appreciate your coming out here on short notice."

"Great to meet *you*," Peter enthused, all smiles and blond curls bobbing as he shook the man's hand vigorously. Jake watched the woman retrieve a television camera from the rear hatch of their van and smirked at how quickly and smoothly Peter took on questions once the camera was rolling. With each question, Peter's answers got longer and more dramatic.

"When that wall of flames leaped across the lake, we knew we were going to die," Peter hammed it up as Jake rolled his eyes and Juanita shot Jake a bemused look. "But the lake gave us a chance. We dived in and clung to the undersides of our raft, linking hands and hoping. We held our breath for as long as we possibly could."

"Is that really how it happened?" Christopher asked Jake.

"That's how it happened," he said, content to let Peter do most of the talking.

"And you, Juanita, what were you thinking as you stood on the edge of that cliff with fire all around you?"

Jake watched Juanita's eyes darken as she relived the moment, but her voice was steady when she replied.

"I heard Jake say he'd rescue me, and I told myself he would. If not for these boys ..." she looked away from the camera and refused to finish the sentence.

"What exactly were you doing in the forest that day?" Christopher asked, but a hovering Forest Service official stepped in abruptly and said, "Those are all the questions these kids want to take for today. We'll have a further report for you in an hour."

The reporter hesitated but obediently lowered his mike and nodded to the camerawoman.

"Hey, can I hold the mike for a minute, just for fun?" Peter's voice begged.

Jake watched Christopher smile, wink at Meredith, and hand over the mike.

"Good evening, viewers. This is Peter Montpetit in Winthrop, Washington, bringing you on-the-spot coverage of the aftermath of the Pasayten Wilderness's most devastating forest fire in history. Here with me today are two youths who escaped the inferno by the skin of their teeth ..."

"'Skin of their teeth' is a cliché, Peter, but you have good eye contact with the camera and your voice projects well," Christopher said as Jake and Juanita exchanged laughing glances. "When you get back to

Seattle, give me a call and I'll give you a tour of the KOMO-TV studios, okay?"

Jake watched Peter's eyes go wide.

"Seriously?"

"Seriously," he said, handing Peter his business card.

Peter held it up as if it were a thousand-dollar bill.

Meredith lowered the camera, patted Peter on the back, and said, "You want that clip? I was rolling, you know."

"You bet!" Peter enthused, turning to Jake with such excitement that Jake backed away for fear Peter was going to hug him.

"Well, guys," Juanita said, trying to herd the boys away from Christopher and Meredith, "we're still meeting to go biking tomorrow, right?"

"We've got bikes for you," her grandfather inserted with a big smile. "And I figure I don't have to worry about Juanita when she's with you two."

"She's showing us Winthrop's best urban riding and jumps," Jake told him.

"That's right, but you two have to take off now," Juanita said in an urgent whisper, glancing behind her. "You have to get back to the house to meet Ron. He's probably waiting there for you, since he left my house just as I got called up here, and I told him we wouldn't be long."

Jake's eyes grew wide. "Ron? Ron is in Winthrop?"

"Who's Ron?" came the reporter's voice behind them.

Juanita turned to the man. "A friend of ours, no one of interest to you." She turned back to Jake and Peter. "He'll tell you his story himself. I promised not to beat him to it. He's here to deliver our checks to us personally."

"Juanita, how could you not …" Jake began, but stopped as he saw Christopher pull out a notebook and the Forest Service official give both him and the reporter a threatening look. Juanita winked at him as if to say, "Too many ears; that's why."

"Right. Well, see you tomorrow for biking, Juanita. Talk to you tonight, too."

"Good idea," she replied with another wink. And with that, she hopped onto her bike, turned, and rode off, leaving the boys staring after her.

Peter extended a hand to Christopher and then to Meredith. "Well, we've gotta go. See you back in Seattle."

"Thanks for the interview," they said.

"Thank *you*."

Jake watched Paul Montpetit, who'd been chatting with a ranger for the past five minutes, scratch his head as the boys raced to his car and leaped in. "What's your hurry, boys?" he said as he joined them at the car. "Grandma won't have supper ready for another couple of hours."

"Expecting a visitor," Jake replied, smiling broadly.

"Is that so?" Mr. Montpetit replied, tugging on his mustache, eyebrows raised. He hustled into the driver's seat and started the car with a roar.

As the car drew up to the house, Jake noted the familiar, beat-up white pickup truck in their driveway, tarp fastened tightly over the back. Checking that no one was in the cab, Jake sprinted up the front steps.

"Oh, hello, Jake and Peter," Trish Montpetit called from the kitchen in a voice that struck Jake as nervous. "Come on back to the patio. Mr. Gabanna just arrived."

Jake strode through the house as if pulled by a wire. When he reached the patio, Jake watched Ron stand, a warm grin stretched across a bruised face. The guide held his big arms out, and Jake walked over to embrace him just as Peter and Mr. Montpetit stepped onto the flagstones.

"I've put some glasses of iced tea and lemon squares on the patio table," Mrs. Montpetit said, moving toward her husband. "Grandpa and I will be in the family room if you need us." She twisted her hands in her apron, then looked to Peter's grandfather for guidance.

"Yes, we'll let you be for a while," he ruled, drawing

her into the house after surveying Ron from head to toe. "We're only a shout away," he added as he turned and led his wife through the house.

Jake, arm's length from Ron now, looked at the guide. His hair was freshly washed, he was wearing clean new clothes, but both eyes were underscored by crescents of black and blue, and his jaw line glowed purple and green. Jake sat down on a patio chair across from where Ron stood.

Peter hung back as Jake and Ron picked up a lemon square each. For a moment, silence hung in the afternoon's heat. Ron sank into a patio chair, sipped his iced tea, and turned gentle eyes on each of the boys in turn. He pushed two envelopes toward them. "Your pay. I heard all about your forest fire escape from Juanita. I'd been worried sick since the news of the fire first broke. Good thinking, goin' onto the lake. Knew you two had good heads on you. Lucky for you that Juanita had that raft, and lucky for her that she had you."

Jake and Peter nodded dumbly.

"Where should I start?" Ron finally asked.

"From the beginning," Peter suggested.

"Right. Guess that'd be a sensible place." He sighed. "Laszlo and Hank never had permission to build a bike trail across the border. They told me they did, offered me very big money upfront to build it, told me not to ask questions or discuss it with a soul. They assigned me two laborers on the Canadian side, and told me to hire two more from the American side to help me finish it by a certain deadline. Part of the deal was also storing a fleet of bikes in my garage for them."

Peter moved forward and sat down on the edge of a lawn chair. "You never questioned the permit part?"

Ron's eyes met his. "No more than you did at first. I liked the money being offered more than the smell of things, but I did what they suggested: asked no questions. I didn't know the two slackers they assigned me were Laszlo's nephews. I didn't know Laszlo would take big exception to my firing them and bringing you two in for the last few days of work. I just wanted to get the job done on time, and those two nephews weren't gonna get us there." He stirred the ice in his glass with a long spoon from the tray.

"So, Laszlo and Hank didn't know you'd hired us till they came up the mountain to check on you?" Jake asked.

"That's right. And they didn't tell me the permit wasn't all the way through till I'd done a large chunk of the trail, not long before I fired the nephews. I chose to believe them that the permit was *almost* through, and I carried on."

He paused again, took a swig of his iced tea, not looking at either boy.

"I lied to you, Juanita, and her grandfather about running the tours myself, as you know. I didn't feel like telling you about Hank and Laszlo at first. I'm sorry about that. But I had a sense that something was fishy, and I guess I was trying to protect you. When Peter thought he was being stalked by a cougar, I figured it might be Laszlo comin' to check on my change of laborers. I was right, and we had an argument in the woods, where I said he should be happy the trail was getting done, never mind by whom, and I told him the story I'd made up to bring you boys and my American workers on board." Ron went quiet for a moment. Jake watched as Peter shifted in his lawn chair, his face tense.

"So there wasn't a cougar?" Peter asked.

"No. Laszlo made it clear he didn't like you kids being brought in without his permission, and he commented on Peter sneakin' into my tent, but he stalked off and let me be. Or so I thought. So I went lookin' for dry cougar scat to cover my absence — not that a cougar lecture wasn't a good thing for you kids to have, anyhow." A flicker of a smile crossed his face, then turned to a scowl.

"Didn't figure on Laszlo continuing to spy; didn't count on him deciding Peter might know what was going down; didn't anticipate Laszlo and Hank" — Ron paused and ran a finger down the bruised side of his face — "giving me an enforced day off, so to speak, with handcuffs and all, so as to determine for themselves what you knew. I could tell Hank wanted no part of that bit, but he was scared of crossing Laszlo."

"What about that note?" Jake inserted. "They wrote it?"

"They wrote a note for me," Ron confirmed.

Jake glanced at Ron's wrists, saw they wore green and yellow bruises. "Are those from the handcuffs?" he asked, wincing. Ron nodded.

For the first time, Ron stood up and began pacing, then stopped beside Peter and looked down on him. "I never reckoned on Peter here puttin' things together faster 'n me." As Peter squirmed a little, Ron laid a hand on Peter's shoulders. "You're too darn smart for your own good," he said. "But at least you got street smarts and survival instincts to go with your suspicious mind."

Peter smiled uncertainly.

Ron produced a sardonic grin at that, then moved over to Jake, laid a hand on Jake's head. "If Jake hadn't said the words 'drug running' aloud, I think Laszlo and Hank would've stayed hidden, and I had a story ready about how a bike crash had roughed up my face and wrists and kept me from getting supplies. But that's not how things worked out."

Now it was Jake's turn to squirm. "I'm … sorry, Ron. That was really … stupid." He glanced at Peter, who was staring at Ron's wrists.

"When Peter escaped Hank, I figured you boys had a chance, so I went for Laszlo. It was risky, and maybe I shouldn't have, but it's not like I had much time to think things through. And anyway, it kind of worked out."

"How *did* it work out?" Jake asked softly. "We've been guessing for days."

Ron finished off his iced tea, turned to Peter, and said, "You got anything stronger than iced tea in this house?" Peter smiled, stepped into the kitchen, and returned with a can of beer.

"Now we're talkin'," Ron said, peeling back the tab and taking a swallow. "Just a little, since I'm drivin'." He eyed Peter. "Laszlo worked me over pretty good and fast, slapped his stupid handcuffs back on me, and threw my bike into the creek. But he was in a hurry to go after you, so that's how he left me. I fetched my bike back up, even with the cuffs on, and started down the trail till I ran into Hank walkin' in my direction, carrying his bike with a bent-up rim in one arm."

"'Cause the other arm was broken, right?" Jake asked.

"No, not his arm, his wrist," Ron replied. "He tells me Laszlo has crashed in a ravine; he's begging me to help. He's pretty shook up, not interested in pursuing you rascals at all."

"Did you wonder where we were then?" Jake asked.

"Escaped, that's all I knew, and that was how it was s'posed to be. I figured somehow you'd make it across the border."

"So you helped Laszlo?" Peter said.

Ron nodded. "First, Hank got the handcuffs off me using our tools. Then we grabbed some ropes and returned to the ravine and climbed down it."

"Did you ever consider just leaving Laszlo there?" Peter asked.

Ron squinted at Peter. "Hank made it clear Laszlo was in rough shape. I'd never have left him there to die. That's against any code I live by." He eyed Peter sternly as if reprimanding him for asking.

"What sort of rough shape?" Jake was feeling impatient to know all the details.

Ron hung his head. "A broken leg, broken hip, and shattered collar bone."

Jake had been expecting something like that, but found himself drawing in his breath slowly.

"How on earth did you get him out of there?" Peter asked.

Ron ran his hands through his hair. "Took us a long time, but we rigged up a stretcher from sticks, rope, and clothing, and hauled him up in stages, Hank with his one good arm."

"I'm impressed," Peter muttered. "Couldn't believe it when I looked in the ravine that night with my headlamp and saw he was gone. Why didn't you bike out and get a helicopter to lift him out?"

"Thought about that, but the weather had turned; it was cloudy and thundering, and I didn't trust the creek to not come up if it rained. We knew we could get him back to camp to care for him overnight without too much trouble if we could get him out of the ravine."

"And then?" Jake asked.

"Next morning, which was Friday, the moment it was light enough, I left Hank tending Laszlo and whipped down to Keremeos to order him a medical helicopter."

"You trusted Hank and Laszlo to stay put?"

Ron guffawed at this. "They weren't goin' nowhere, and with Laszlo in no position to bully Hank, Hank had already told me he was ready to cut his losses."

"What does that mean, cut his losses?" Jake asked.

"It means he knew I was going to report them to the authorities and he'd decided to cooperate to minimize whatever trouble he was going to get into."

"So, then what?" Peter pushed.

"A helicopter evacuated Laszlo to hospital, and they say he'll recover. Fully enough to probably serve some time in jail for 'intention to traffic,' they told me. The fact that he'd already ordered in drugs from Colombia will seal his fate on that count, most likely.

At least, that's what a friend who knows about legal stuff told me. Hank got his wrist treated, then we turned ourselves in at the police station. Since it was Friday afternoon by then, and the only official available to interrogate us had to travel from somewhere else on Monday, they threw us in jail for the weekend."

Ron paused long and hard there. "Boys, don't you ever, ever get yourselves thrown in jail, even for a day."

"But they let you go with no charges?" Jake knew it was a dumb question since Ron was here with them and had been able to cross the border.

"Yes," he said, raising a hand and bringing it down fondly on Jake's head. He swigged back more beer and continued. "I got questioned real hard. Then they let me out, no charges or nothin', partly because another police team was questioning you and Juanita down here same time and you guys were vouching for me." He coughed. "They let Hank out on bail at the same time. The courts will decide how much, if any time he'll do in jail — less than Laszlo likely, since he cooperated and wasn't the ringleader. I'll have lots of testifying to do when Hank and Laszlo's case comes to court. You might, too."

"And you drove straight down here and found us through Juanita?" Jake asked.

Ron nodded. "While I was in jail, I heard the news about the forest fire. I remembered Jake telling me about Peter having a grandpa in Winthrop, and I decided that's where you'd come out. Could've called your mom to make sure," he added, looking at Jake, "but didn't think she wanted to hear from me at that point."

"You probably got that right," Jake replied.

"Never occurred to me that you'd actually run into Juanita and José and know who they were," Ron said, eyebrows raised toward Peter.

"But we did," Peter said slyly.

"Anyhow, I drove down here this morning, and Juanita told me everything. Even if you hadn't met her, though, it wouldn't have been hard to find your place once I asked in town about a man who was one of the first smokejumpers."

Peter beamed, then picked up the white envelopes and frowned. "How'd you have money to pay us, after all this?"

"Laszlo paid me for half the trail-building before I started. He and Hank also paid for all the bikes in my garage in cash, and when Hank and I talked, we decided I'd sell them and split the money three ways: for me, and for Hank's and Laszlo's families to help them cope while they're in jail."

Jake was stunned by this for a second, before he remembered that Ron himself had a family badly affected by a dad going to jail.

"All except for the three full-suspension bikes," Ron said, looking at each boy in turn. "I fixed Laszlo's, which fared better than him in the fall, and repaired Hank's. I gave mine to Juanita this morning, and Hank and I agreed the other two should go to you two. They ain't new anymore, but like I said, I fixed 'em up good, and that's a promise."

"Whoa, thanks," Peter said, face lit up.

"Not sure we should take them or the money," Jake suddenly spoke up. "Doesn't seem right."

"You will take both," Ron boomed with a sparkle in his eyes. "It's honest pay for an honest week's hard work, not to mention a bonus for danger pay."

Peter smiled as he tucked his envelope into his back jeans pocket and watched Jake reach slowly for his.

"That's quite a story," Peter said, leaning back in his lawn chair and gazing warmly at Ron.

"It is, and it could've had lots of worse endings," Ron said, nodding. "Now, you boys want a ride back up to Canada, or you got transportation to wherever you're goin' next?"

Jake and Peter looked at each another. "We're biking with Juanita tomorrow. She knows some good urban around here."

"That she does," Ron said emphatically.

"Will you come with us?" the boys asked together.

"Nah, thanks anyway. What will you two do then?"

"Peter's grandpa is driving us to Peter's house in Seattle the day after tomorrow," Peter started.

"And my mom and sister are coming down to Seattle for a little holiday with Peter's parents," Jake broke in. "We haven't had a family holiday since, well, since forever."

"Sounds good, and that reminds me," Ron said, leaning over to unzip his dusty backpack and pull out a jar and box. "Hope you don't mind I added half a dozen to your collection. Wasn't me, really. My sister was real into catchin' them yesterday afternoon when I showed her your get-up, especially knowing you helped get me outta jail. She did that while I was watching my nephew, not that he takes much watching at his age."

His face turned soft and he blushed full red. "Keremeos butterflies. Souvenir of your Cathedral Provincial Park adventure. Come by to collect more anytime, kids." He rose and busied himself with zipping his pack back up.

"Thought you were never in one place long enough to be counted on for stuff like that," Jake said, softly. Peter stood and moved toward Ron as if determined not to miss shaking Ron's hand.

Ron, without warning, picked Peter up and gave him a bear hug, then put the startled boy down on his feet and tousled his hair. "True enough. But for you and Peter, now, that would be a different story entirely. Stay honest, boys." And with that, he clapped each on their back, tipped his baseball cap, and was gone.

As Jake heard his truck pull out of the driveway, he and Peter suddenly scrambled up and out the door, only to trip over two nearly brand-new, top-of-the-line, full-suspension bikes, leaning up against the front porch.

They stepped forward to touch them as a billow of dust rose from the road.

"Where the heck did those come from?" Mr. Montpetit asked as he appeared behind them.

"Oh, my," Mrs. Montpetit said, hand over her mouth.

"From Ron. Awesome bikes," Peter said reverently.

"Made for surviving," Jake said.

Acknowledgments

My two most valued collaborators on this book were downhill mountain bikers Jeremy Withers (my son, age sixteen) and Cam McRae, who is editor of Jake's, Peter's, and Jeremy's favorite free-ride website, www.nsmb.com (North Shore Mountain Biking). Tyler Lawson and Robin Munshaw also helped with mountain biking expertise, and thirteen-year-old Calvin Bueckert of Pinawa, Manitoba, suggested the book's title. I'm also indebted to former wildfire-fighter Noel Hendrickson; former Cathedral Provincial Park ranger Jen Picker; Paul Terbasket of Cathedral Lakes Lodge; Royal Canadian Mounted Police officer Sheilah Roy; lawyers Letitia Sears and Bani Dheer; Mark McLennan of the adventure company B.C. Extreme (www.bcextreme.bc.ca); television cameraman Peter Rummel; Sandra Benassini for Hispanic perspective; and writer/friend Shannon Young for reading an early version of the manuscript.

As always, I'm privileged to acknowledge the talented and dedicated team at Whitecap Books, without whom this series would not exist — especially my editors/mentors/coaches Carolyn Bateman and Robin Rivers and proofreader Elizabeth McLean. And last but definitely not least, ongoing thanks to my literary agent Leona Trainer and my speaking tours agent Chris Patrick.

ISBN 1-55285-510-4

Arch rivals and sometimes friends Peter and Jake are delighted to be part of a whitewater-rafting trip. But after a series of disasters leaves the group stranded in the wilderness, it's up to them to confront the dangerous rapids to search for help. This is the first title in the extreme outdoor sports series by Pam Withers.

Jake, Peter, and Moses are looking forward to heli-skiing and snowboarding in the backcountry near Whistler. But just after they're dropped off on a mountain peak, bad weather closes in and a helicopter crashes. It's up to them to rescue any survivors and overcome avalanches, hypothermia, and wild animals to make their way to safety.

ISBN 1-55285-530-9

ISBN 1-55285-604-6

It's summer vacation for best friends Peter and Jake, and when they're invited to help develop a mountain bike trail west of the Canadian Rockies, they can't believe their luck. But as they start working hard in an isolated park, the boys sense that something's not right. Join the boys as they plunge into the mountain-biking descent of their lives.